HUNGER OF THE ABYSS

BOOK I

CAMBION

LUKE HOFFMAN

Join the mailing list at HungerOfTheAbyss.com for updates, extras, merchandise, and a free novella.

CONTENTS

ACKNOWLEDGMENTS

Thank you to all the amazing people who made this book a reality, from the host of advance readers who gave such great feedback, to my wife, Andrea, who helped bring Zilzina to life.

Special thanks to Ally, my editor, and Catherine, without whom this book may never have been written.

CHAPTER I

Zilzina's boots crushed into fresh snow, finding the hardened dirt packed underneath as she stalked through the wintry forest of Frigia. Her sharp, elven eyes were alert, pupils dilated for the hunt. A lesser devil was her prey–not as powerful as a full demon, but plenty dangerous, especially to the villagers it had been terrorizing.

The monster had run rampant in a small village up north for several days until she'd arrived. Zilzina had taken the hellspawn by surprise, wounding it and driving it into the forest. Though the meager bounty the villagers offered her to finish the jobs wasn't even worth returning to collect, she decided to track it down all the same.

There were other things the devil could help her with.

Moving through the deep snow was difficult. Fresh powder spilled into the hunter's boots with each step.

However, the gleaming frost did have one benefit: clearly showing the devil's erratic tracks as it bounded through the woods. Large, trailing dark splotches had long since stopped–demons healed much more quickly than most races–but small droplets of its infernal blood still shone black on the white surface. Still though, Zilzina was not stupid enough to underestimate the creature. For all she knew, the obvious tracks were a trap, meant to lure her into a false sense of security as the devil circled back around.

Eventually, the trail turned east, toward Miesot, one of the two major cities of the Frigian territory. That was strange, considering demons would generally stay in rural areas. It should be heading deeper into the forest, where it was less likely to encounter an Imperial patrol or a hunter, though the number of hunters was dwindling these days. There was something off about the devil's movements.

"Shit," Zilzina hissed, breaking into a jog. It wasn't laying out obvious traps, she realized. It was wounded and knew it couldn't escape without replenishing its strength. And what was the quickest way to replenish that strength? Feeding. Only a panicking devil would run straight in the direction of the city. Zilzina had to stop it before it took more innocent lives.

As twilight came on, she hurried after the obvious tracks. Even in the fading dusk, the hunter's vision was sharp–her eyes gleamed like a cat's in the low light. Off to the side, a second trail broke to the right, signaled by a bright red stain. She stopped and touched the snow. It was still warm. Wiping her hand on her thigh, Zilzina considered the diverging path.

Could it be that the devil was able to create a fake trail? No, there hadn't been enough time. There must have been more than one. How had she missed that? Sloppy. But which way to go? The blood was not a good sign. Bright, like a human's. If the devil she had wounded was feeding…

A scream split the chilled air from the right, bloodstained path.

Zilzina sprang into action without a second thought, sprinting toward the fading cries for help. Her pointed ears pricked up as she continued to navigate by following the piercing sounds. Some minutes later, once the screams had died out, she was able to follow the scent of fresh blood–not an elven trait, but one she possessed nonetheless. It led her to a rugged log cabin nestled in a hidden meadow. At another time, it may have been beautiful, picturesque even, with its frozen pond and stack of logs for the fire.

As it was, the scene inspired more horror than beauty. A trail of fresh blood led in through the front door, barely hanging from its hinges as if it had been wrenched free with great force. A sickening crunching and chewing sound was the only thing Zilzina heard from within, punctuated by occasional sobs. Slowing her pace, Zilzina stepped stealthily toward the cabin, peering inside. It was a small, one-room affair. Although it was dark, she could see the devil near the door, feasting upon a mangled woman. Across the room, in the corner near a large bed, sat a girl, balled up and shaking with fear.

The demon was so engrossed in his feeding that he didn't notice Zilzina approaching until the floorboard creaked loudly. He lifted his head and glared, his animalistic features sending a shudder down the hunter's spine as no other creature could. Smiling fiendishly, the devil rose from his knees to his full height. The blood of his victim was smeared across his face, a stark contrast against the sickly pale skin, as incongruous as the bloodstains upon the snow outside the cabin.

Zilzina wondered briefly if she had ever looked like that.

"Ah, a second course before dessert," the devil chuckled, glancing from Zilzina to the girl in the corner. It was too dark to make out her features, but Zilzina could tell from smell alone that she wasn't human. Several embers wafted slowly through the air near her, probably from the cooking fire though the hearth was dark.

"You're going to have to wait just a little longer," the devil said to her, turning back to Zilzina and growling threateningly as he lunged. His speed was more than she'd anticipated, much quicker than most lesser devils, but it was no match for Zilzina's experience and hunter's instincts. She dodged nimbly out of the way.

Nothing would stop her from finding Sannazu. Nothing would stop her from ending that hellspawn and her curse with one fell stroke.

The hunter drew her dagger and dodged another swipe, dragging the weapon across the devil's side in a flash of silver. The monster shrieked again, this time in pain. Silver was the weakness of all hellspawn and dealt grievous injuries that they could not heal quickly from. Many unwary villagers had been taken by surprise when a demon had allowed them to strike it with a pitchfork or a wood axe in order to get close, only to realize that it had little effect.

This wound was shallow, however, and the devil was reappraising his foe. Zilzina moved in for her own attack this time, lunging at the beast, but it retreated to the other side of the cabin. It was dangerously close to the girl now. She had to keep it occupied. Her blows were fast but the devil, now totally engrossed in defense, skillfully dodged them, though he was running out of room in the small cabin.

"I'm not going to fall to a mere girl!" he roared.

To Zilzina's surprise, large, batlike wings sprang from the devil's shoulders, cracking and stretching sickly as they expanded. Not many devils evolved to the point of having wings–this one must have devoured scores of people. Perhaps she had underestimated this quarry.

He whirled about, using the razor-sharp wings as weapons. In a single deft movement, Zilzina dropped to her knees and rolled backward. The devil stayed on her, pressing forward, knocking the silver dagger from her hand and grabbing her by the throat.

"You really thought you could walk out of here alive?" he laughed, tightening his grip and drawing a grunt of paint from Zilzina. "You must be joking!"

He threw Zilzina so forcefully that she crashed through the small cabin's only window, splintering the shutters in all directions. She bounced into a snow drift, vision exploding with blinding pain. Suddenly, a crash split the air as the devil burst through the cabin's thatched roof, flying over to the hunter with a few powerful flaps of his wings.

"Ah, aren't you a pretty one, even for an elf," he purred, eyeing the dagger and tossing it aside. "You're a hunter? What are you going to do without your silver?"

Zilzina managed to get up. Her features set in a stern, concentrated mask, devoid of any emotion that might betray her next move, and she limped towards the monster. The devil smiled and extended his wings menacingly.

"You think that's my only silver?" Zilzina asked, donning a smirk of her own. She drew forth an ivory-handled, tri-barreled pistol from its strap within her cloak.

The devil's eyes widened and he lunged again for the hunter, but it was too late. Her first shot went through his left arm. The devil shrieked in pain and stumbled back. His next movements were a blur as he tried to throw Zilzina's aim off, but more shrieks followed as the subsequent two shots found purchase in his tough, pale skin.

He crashed into the side of the cabin, panting. "How?!" he roared, pulling one of the silver bullets from his chest and flinging it away with a hiss.

"You're not nearly as fast, or as clever, as you think you are," Zilzina replied casually, though strain from her injuries edged its way into her voice. "The movements are quite predictable."

"What kind of an elf are you?" the devil growled. He had taken the stance of an injured animal, plotting his escape but ready to take the defensive at a moment's notice.

"The kind that really hates demons."

Gritting his monstrous teeth, the devil spread its wings and attempted to take flight.

"Not this time," the hunter murmured. She quickly removed a dark whip from her hip, cracking it so that the runes in its handle glowed orange in the twilight. With a second swing, it wrapped around the devil's leg, smoking wherever it made contact.

If it was left to a contest of strength, the devil would win.

But it wasn't.

"Wrap," Zilzina said to the whip. Its runes glowed brighter as it stretched beyond its length to entangle the demon, binding him tightly and forcing his wings together. The hellspawn crashed unceremoniously to the ground with a wet crack.

"What the hell is this?!" he gasped, struggling against his bonds.

Zilzina reloaded her pistol slowly, each of the three silvered bullets pressed firmly into its barrel.

"Wait!" the devil pleaded. "I can be of service to you."

"Where can I find Sannazu?" Zilzina asked. She clicked the pistol's firing pin and leveled the barrels at her prey's head.

The devil tried to speak, but like every other demon to whom Zilzina had asked this question, he was unable to get a single word out.

"Cat got your tongue?"

"I... I can't even say his name," the demon whined.

"Then you're of no use," Zilzina replied and fired all three barrels. The devil's head exploded in a mist of gore. "Enjoy hell."

Finally, the hunter let out a breath. Her wrist was broken, of that she was sure, and her ribs weren't feeling so hot either. At least three days to fully heal, though a bit of demon's blood would speed that up. Stepping past the devil's carcass and into the cabin, Zilzina found the girl covering the dead woman, probably her mother, with a sheet.

"Are you okay?" Zilzina asked, realizing too late that the answer was obvious.

The girl was weeping and turned around slowly.

"What the hell are you?" gasped Zilzina, reloading her pistol and leveling it in a well-practiced motion. Now that she had moved closer, Zilzina could see who she had saved. The girl had dusky red scales for skin and two small horns. Her black eyes peered out fearfully from behind raven hair.

The very description of a demon although her form seemed underdeveloped.

The girl rose, the tears streaming down her face steaming in the cold air. Zilzina lowered her aim, perhaps because of how innocent and helpless the girl looked, though she kept the pistol in hand.

"That's... that's enough," said the demon hunter. When the girl wouldn't stop crying, she holstered the gun and approached her. "Ok, it's away, see? Okay?"

The girl made no response. She seemed too deep in grief to even take notice of Zilzina. The hunter didn't completely let her guard down, but this girl did not seem to be a threat–not at the moment in any case.

Carefully, Zilzina placed her hand on the girl's downturned head. "Was she your mother?"

The girl nodded, her sobs breaking out in a new burst of steam.

How horrible it must have been to watch her mother eaten before her very eyes. Why were they so far out in the forest alone?

"Is it just you and your mother that live here?" Zilzina prodded, eliciting a nod from the girl. "No other family?"

The girl looked up finally, gazing out through the door past Zilzina to the devil's corpse that lay still smoldering in the snow.

Zilzina's eyes widened in realization. "You're a cambion," she said more than asked. She stepped back to get a better look at the girl now that her sobbing had lessened.

"Is that... what you call a half-demon?" the girl asked.

Zilzina nodded.

"Then I guess I'm a cambion," replied the girl. She looked down at her mother, covered now with a sheet that was soaking through with blood. "My mother kept me hidden for as long as I can remember." She paused and suddenly grasped her stomach, retching a bit. Zilzina guessed she had reached her limit staying in the same room as her mother's body.

Shit. Realization dawned on Zilzina that this was not the demon she had been tracking. For one, it wasn't even injured, and beyond that, it was far more powerful than the fiend she had sparred with earlier. The other was still in flight, probably toward a village where it could feed and heal.

"I have to go," the hunter said to the girl.

"Oh," the girl replied. Her face grew sullen and she bowed her head again.

In a moment of tenderness, Zilzina put a hand on her shoulder. *What am I doing? I shouldn't be weak like this...* "What's your name?"

"Autumn."

"Okay, Autumn. You have two choices," Zilzina replied coolly. "You can either run north to the village or you can wait here until I return."

"I want to go with you," Autumn said.

"Not an option," Zilzina snapped. "You would only slow me down." She slipped a small flashlight out of her pocket and handed it to Autumn. "I'm pretty sure your lamps are busted so take this just in case I'm not back before dark or you decide to head off to the village on your own."

The hunter took a deep breath and turned away, ignoring the slight pang in her heart the girl's pleading face caused. Autumn would be fine. The devil tearing its way toward the nearest settlement took priority. She would find it and be back here in a flash; likely the girl would already have left on her own to the safety of the village.

With a nod, Zilzina sprinted out of the cabin at preternatural speed. It was one of the perks of her curse, although the need to consume demon's blood regularly made it not particularly worth it. Her back hurt and her broken wrist was practically screaming at her, but there was no time to rest. She ran onward, seeking further prey amidst the wintry forest.

After a good hour, or what seemed an eternity, she caught scent of the devil.

The trail had been erratic, but eventually, the beast had found a logging camp. Just ahead, she smelled more than saw the devil as he stalked a dwarven woodcutter out late. He was hard at work at the edge of a clearing littered with fresh tree stumps. In the distance, the light of a campfire cast an orange glow in the chilled forest, shadows dancing off of tents, trees, and piles of logs.

The unsuspecting dwarf had no idea what watched just beyond the shadows' edge. He was loading short cuts from a felled tree onto his sled, just about to head back to the warmth and comfort of the camp, when the devil attacked.

Zilzina vowed to get there first. Enough innocent blood had been spilled that day.

She tore through the clearing, treading easily across the tree stumps, dagger in hand. The beast's claws were mere inches away from the dwarf's head when the silver crescent of her strike tore through its neck, sending a dark blood spray across the pristine snow.

The devil's head rolled lazily to a halt at the logger's feet. He looked down at it and screamed. "What the hell?" he shouted, dropping his sled and running back toward the camp. "Demon!" he screamed again, only this time he was looking at Zilzina, devil's blood sprayed across her unnaturally pale features. Already shouts and clamor could be heard from the camp as they rustled up a hunting party.

"You're welcome," Zilzina muttered, grabbing the devil's arm and dragging it away with her. It wasn't the dwarf's fault–she knew her appearance was unnerving, especially when she needed to feed. Her features were mostly elven but there was something not quite right in them, something... demonic.

Whether she really was a demon or not, Zilzina didn't know, but she was cursed to drink their blood either way. Wearing a hood in public had become a habit after one too many altercations. Her silver hair was no giveaway, many elves had silver hair, but the pointed teeth were certainly abnormal and the sickly pale skin didn't help. Not to mention her eyes, glowing violet and rimmed in silver. Again, not quite demonic but not a trait many shared.

In this day and age, most people were suspicious of anything out of the ordinary.

Sannazu's curse had ruined her life. After he had killed her family all those years ago, he had left her to suffer the hunger of his final joke. "Little one," he had said in a deep voice, a forked tongue flicking over his pointed teeth. "Feel my pain. Feel my hunger."

Zilzina turned to the decapitated devil, dropping it into the snow once they were far enough away from the logging camp. A part of her, perhaps all that was left of that little elven girl cursed all those years ago, found what she was to do next repulsive; another part of her, the stronger and more violent part, was nearly overwhelmed by a desire to consume the devil's blood.

Veins stood taut in the hunter's neck as she bent down slowly to drink from the corpse's bleeding stump. As always, she licked and slurped patiently, unwilling to give herself over completely to the feeding, as the demons did. She may be cursed but she would not become wholly like them.

CHAPTER II

Autumn sat on the chopping stump outside her cabin. Despite the winter chill, she wasn't cold. She'd never really been cold. There was a fire burning within her--she could feel it though, it had never done any harm. The cabin loomed behind, a place that had once offered comfort and warmth now only reminding her of a dead mother and the demon who took her away.

The demon who was her father.

With a cry of anguish, Autumn leapt to her feet and thrust her hands outward, towards the cabin. A bright, hot flame burst forth, strengthened by her scream. It burned hotter and hotter until the entire structure was aflame, a proper burial for her mother. She'd given her life to protect Autumn. Even if her mother had never quite understood what the cambion girl was going through, she had always loved her. When the people of the village had found out about Autumn, her mother had simply packed up their things and told the girl that they were going to move to the forest.

Autumn felt hot tears welling in her eyes again as she watched their house burn. This was all her fault. Why did she have to be this way? Why had the gods destined her for this cruel fate?

Of course she couldn't live among other people, she knew that. They would kill her out of fear, thinking she was a demon like her father. No one would care that she had never harmed anyone. And Autumn couldn't even blame them. Demons only had one instinct: to feed.

The girl felt a few soft snowflakes brush her cheek and evaporate in puffs of steam. It was getting close to morning and the elf hadn't yet returned. She hadn't even asked the hunter's name. As the flurry strengthened, Autumn settled into her favorite nook under the old oak tree beside the frozen pond. She'd wait as long as it took for that elf to return.

She was the only person besides Autumn's mother who'd ever treated her like a person.

The longer she waited, the more afraid Autumn grew that the hunter wouldn't return. Maybe she'd been killed, or worse decided that Autumn wasn't worth coming back for after all. No, she didn't need to decide that. Her promise to return had been a lie all along. Autumn's life was a cruel joke–it was only fitting.

The snow was piling up quickly now, though a zone around the cambion girl was kept clear by her internal heat melting it instantly. "Where is she?" Autumn gritted her teeth and stood, taking the flashlight Zilzina had left out of her pocket and flicking it on. "Oh, forget it, Autumn," she continued to herself, tramping through the thickening blanket of snow, her footprints steaming in the brisk morning air. "She doesn't need someone like you tagging on. Did you think she'd be your nanny?"

The hunter's scent was fading but she could still follow it easily. She would track her down and ask her why she hadn't returned like she promised–and bury her if the worst had happened. Autumn knew following a hunter who was chasing a demon was dangerous, but she didn't particularly care right then. Whatever would happen would happen. Let fate decide.

She wasn't fast, her tracking skills weren't honed like that of a hunter's, but she made steady progress. The flashlight was a godsend. Having grown up in a cabin outside of a rural village, Autumn had rarely even seen a lightbulb much less one that fit in her hand. Whoever this hunter was she'd certainly experienced more of the world than Autumn had.

The cambion's limited experience tracking rabbits and deer with her mother told her she was close. There was a village not too far from here, maybe the hunter had stopped at

HUNGER OF THE ABYSS: CAMBION

an inn to rest. Autumn was just starting to head in that direction when a new scent hit her.

Blood.

Demon blood, entwined with the elf lady's scent. Autumn cursed–she should have noticed it sooner but was too busy being angry at the hunter for not returning. Her tread lightened and she clicked the flashlight off, causing her eyes to shine in the moonlight. She didn't have the same level of night vision as a full demon, but she could see well enough in the dark when need called for it.

Autumn crested a low hill and gasped. The hunter was crouched over the corpse of a headless demon. As the elf turned to look at her, Autumn could feel those glowing, violet eyes burning into her very being. Dropping the body, the hunter wiped dark blood from her face with a hiss.

"Wait, stop," Zilzina called in a low voice as Autumn took several steps back.

Autumn froze, her heart beating faster and faster. A shiver ran down her spine, though not from the snow–it was the feeling of being the sole object of a predator's gaze. Even when the devil, her father, had attacked she hadn't felt like this.

"Don't run," continued Zilzina, taking a step further. She pulled her hood up but Autumn could still see those bloody fangs glinting in the moonlight.

Like hell she wouldn't run.

Autumn bolted, moving faster than she'd ever moved before. She could feel the fire welling up inside her, driving her screaming limbs into a frenzy she'd never experienced. The girl ran until her legs were shaking and she collapsed in a fresh bank with a hiss of melting snow.

How long before the elf caught her? Had she simply saved her for dessert, like her father? Autumn cursed her own stupidity for thinking the hunter would protect her.

A branch snapped somewhere off to her left. Autumn immediately got to her feet, crouching low and switching the flashlight on. Its beam flickered but a few well-placed smacks and curses brought it back.

"Where are you?" Autumn whispered beneath clenched teeth as she scanned the tree line. Something moved at the edge of the beam, a mere shadow. "Where are you?" Autumn said again, louder this time.

"Here," a deep, feline voice purred in her ear.

Autumn spun around as another devil grabbed at her. They both shrieked, one in fear and the other in the pleasure of the kill. Just as the fiend's claws scraped against scaley flesh, a dark blur tore between them. Zilzina slid through the snow, her silver dagger flashing red in her hand. Autumn and the devil both stumbled backward, away from each other.

"Ok, now run," Zilzina hissed and dashed again toward

her prey.

Autumn didn't think twice. She pushed her aching limbs to move again, her inner fire burning brighter than ever. Embers flew in her wake as the snow melted and the bark of passing trees was singed. The girl looked back, seeing the hunter and devil sparring as they ran in her wake.

When she turned front again, she ran headlong into a tree and fell to the ground. All went black.

***

Autumn opened her eyes slowly. Everything was blurry and her head was throbbing in pain. After a few moments, she could see the dawn sky lightening off to her right. Somewhere nearby a fire crackled.

With a start, she sat up and scanned her surroundings. The elf sat cross legged on the other side of the campfire. Her black coat was gone. Autumn realized that it was underneath her–the hunter had laid it out for the girl to rest on.

"What do you want with me?" Autumn said, scrambling back and finding that she was against a wall. They were in a low cave created by two large boulders pressed against each other. "If you're going to… eat me…"

"Relax, I'm not going to eat you," Zilzina sighed and stoked the fire. "You caused me a lot of trouble tonight, you know."

"Oh, right, sorry," replied Autumn, edging toward the

mouth of the cave. "Anyway, I should be going. Thanks for… killing the…"

"You sprained your ankle," the hunter said without moving. "Not to mention that nasty bump on the head. You need to rest."

Autumn reached down to feel her ankle and hissed with pain. The adrenaline of the moment was wearing off. She slumped to the ground several feet away from her makeshift bed.

"I'm Zilzina," the elf continued and looked to Autumn expectantly. She was obviously exhausted but did her best to smile–it wasn't an expression the hunter often wore. "So are you going to limp out of here? Or do you want some help getting back to bed?"

After a moment the girl replied. "Ok, help me back."

Zilzina stood and walked over to Autumn and put an arm around her and beneath her knees, lifting the cambion easily. She was stronger than she looked. With a little maneuvering, the hunter laid Autumn back down on her coat and sat back down on the other side of the fire. Both of them gazed into its crackling flames for some time before Autumn spoke again.

"You were feeding on a demon," she stated. It wasn't a question.

"Yes," replied Zilzina calmly. Her violet eyes did not seem so threatening now but Autumn couldn't help but remember the feeling they'd instilled in her before.

"You're cursed, aren't you?"

Zilzina looked down and paused. "Why did you follow me?"

"I was scared," Autumn said, wishing now that she'd just waited. She could have saved herself from the headache and the sprain. "I thought you weren't coming back. I... sorry about running like that. I really thought that-"

"It's fine," Zilzina cut her off and laid back, using her small pack as a pillow.

The words only made Autumn feel more guilty. They lay there in silence again for a while. The fire cast dancing shadows across the wall and Zilzina's features. Her pale skin and silver hair made for a jarring sight, even more so with the violet glow from her slitted eyelids, but Autumn decided she was honestly quite beautiful.

"You're staring," the hunter said.

"Well, I don't have much else to do," Autumn huffed and turned over to face the wall.

"You should have stayed at the cabin."

"I burned it down." Autumn could feel a knot forming in her chest but resolved not to cry in front of Zilzina. Not again anyway.

"I see. Then why not head for the village? I'm sure the oni would take you in."

Autumn didn't respond, just shifted a bit to get more comfortable.

"How old are you?" asked Zilzina after a while. The fire was dying out and the embers' glow was fading with the morning light.

"Fourteen I think," Autumn replied. They hadn't kept close track of the calendar, and in Frigia the days were mostly the same with seasons ranging from winter to winter.

"How long have you been hiding?" Zilzina was doing her best to comfort the girl, though this was not her realm of expertise. Taking care of a child on her own? Quite literally the last thing she ever thought she'd be doing.

"I don't know," Autumn said, turning over onto her back like Zilzina. They watched the embers of the dying fire dance across the cave's ceiling. "My mother and I have been on the run for as long as I can remember. There was another cabin last year, and the edge of the village, and even a short time on the outskirts of Miesot with some of our family. We could never stay anywhere for long though. Somehow, he always found us, my father, though I guess that's over now."

"I see," was all the hunter said.

"Well, what about you?" Autumn asked, a bit of annoyance edging into her voice.

"What about me?"

"I've heard there aren't many demon hunters left," the girl

continued. "Do you do it for a bounty?"

"Among other reasons, yes."

Autumn turned her head and glared at the elf. Zilzina did her best to ignore her but even she was not immune. That stare always wore Autumn's mother down, the girl was well practiced in getting her way.

"What?" growled Zilzina. This was exactly why she avoided children–well, usually. Back at Serah's…

"Who cursed you to, you know, eat demons?"

"Sannazu." The answer was curt. Zilzina played idly with her knife.

Autumn edged a little closer. "Who is San-"

"Shh," Zilzina hissed. "Hellspawn can't say that name. It's dangerous. He's strong, even for a demon."

"Ah, ok…"

"I've been hunting him for a long time but it's like he's a ghost. Every time I get close, poof, he's gone."

Autumn could hear the anger Zilzina was holding back. "What will you do when you find him?"

"I'll make him lift the curse. Then I'll kill him," said the elf, and Autumn could've sworn that the violet glow in her eyes flared up briefly.

Scary. "So… how long have you been cursed?"

Zilzina sighed and sat up, rummaging in her pack for something. Pulling out a small container, she walked over and knelt by Autumn.

"Where are you going to search next? How does demon blood taste? I bet it's awful. How many demons have you killed? Where did you learn to fight? Why-"

"No more questions," Zilzina said. She put a palm over Autumn's mouth for emphasis.

The cambion's eyes dropped sullenly but she nodded. Zilzina examined the sprained ankle, eliciting a hiss from the girl as she turned it gently. "This balm will help," she said, unscrewing the container and applying a smelly paste on the dusky red scales of Autumn's ankle.

Autumn couldn't help but think of her mother. Her mother, the woman who had loved her and cared for her. Who would do that now? Would Zilzina stay with her? The girl pinched her own cheeks. She really had to stop almost crying.

After a minute or two, Zilzina stood and put the balm away. "Try to get a few hours of sleep. Once you're up, I'll take you to the village."

Autumn's heart dropped. "What? I don't have anyone there."

Zilzina walked to the cave entrance and looked out at the sun slipping up over the horizon. "That village has a large oni population. Their people have ancient ties to demons, one of them will understand. Hopefully."

"Hopefully?" repeated Autumn spitefully.

"I'll make something work."

"I don't want to make something work. I want to stay with you!"

"Autumn, I can't be that person for you," Zilzina sighed. She settled against the wall, still looking away, out through the cave's opening.

"It's because I'm a demon, isn't it? You hate me," Autumn choked.

"You know that's not true."

"Whatever," Autumn replied. She sat up and pulled her dress, now dirty and torn from the action the night before, off over her head.

"What are you doing?" Zilzina asked, turning around with another sigh. "Oh, you have a tail."

"I do," Autumn said matter-of-factly and laid back down to sleep in her underclothes, which her mother had modified to allow the short, vestigial tail to pass through. She always felt more comfortable sleeping this way. "I'm going to sleep, leave me alone."

Zilzina fell silent for the rest of the morning, letting the girl sleep longer than she'd intended. Autumn knew she was being harsh, and that the hunter was doing her best, but it didn't matter. It was like what she wanted didn't even matter and the thought of returning to a village made her stomach turn.

***

It was almost noon by the time they set out back for the village. Autumn hadn't said a word to Zilzina, and she didn't plan on it.

That was until her stomach spoke for her, growling loudly.

"Are you hungry?" Zilzina asked finally.

Autumn flushed, as much as a crimson scaled cambion could, and turned away, cursing her stomach silently.

"You should have said something," the hunter continued wryly.

"There's a rabbit hiding over there," Autumn broke her silence at last. She pointed to a bush some distance off to their right.

Zilzina drew her silver dagger and tossed it skillfully in the air, catching it again after a full rotation.

"How big do you suppose?"

"You can't miss it," said Autumn, noticing large pawprints near the bush.

Zilzina nodded and threw the knife with deadly speed. It flew straight through the bush. The rabbit leapt out and darted away, leaving a thin trail of blood in the snow.

"Huh, I guess you can miss it," Autumn taunted.

Zilzina cursed and ran after the rabbit. Autumn was laughing with her hand over her mouth as she watched the elf chase the injured creature.

Several minutes later, with the use of what Zilzina explained was an enchanted whip, their lunch was secured.

"So, are you done giving me the silent treatment?" Zilzina asked as she built up a fire.

Autumn was skinning the rabbit in the way her mother had taught her. Truthfully, she was tired of trying to ignore Zilzina. It wasn't in her nature to be quiet. She was constantly asking her mother questions, who was much more patient than Zilzina was.

"We're halfway to the village, I would think by now-"

"How did you get an enchanted whip?" Autumn interrupted. Magic was rare and its practitioners were becoming less and less common. It had once been more widespread but as technology continued to replace its primary uses, those who practiced the arcane arts were increasingly viewed with suspicion.

"Someone very close to me enchanted it," Zilzina said, running her fingers over the familiar runes on the whip's handle.

"Well that answer is boring," Autumn replied and hissed when she accidentally cut her finger with Zilzina's dagger.

"Shit, be careful." Zilzina hurried over and took Autumn's hand. "The silver will hurt you more than most."

"It's okay, it's just a scratch."

A drop of blood welled up on Autumn's finger and fell to the pristine snow below. Zilzina fell quiet, watching it closely.

"Zilzina?" continued Autumn. "Are you okay?"

She could've sworn a vein appeared below the elf's eye, but it disappeared when she blinked.

"Fine," Zilzina said quickly, turning to the rabbit and taking over preparation. Once their lunch was cooked and their meal was finished, they set off again toward the village.

"So, you don't carry much with you," Autumn noted as they trudged along.

"Nope, slows me down," Zilzina replied, adjusting her small pack.

"Do you always hunt to eat then?"

"Mostly. Normal food only holds me over so long," replied the hunter.

"Ah, yes. Right. And how do you make money?"

"I'm a bounty hunter."

"Sounds like a shaky job."

"I'm beginning to regret giving you the go ahead to speak again," Zilzina lamented, drawing a giggle from Autumn.

A gust of wind brought a familiar, sickening scent to Autumn's nostrils. "Zilzina," the girl said, stopping in her tracks.

"I know, keep moving."

A while later Zilzina spoke up again. "A demon and two

lesser devils yesterday. Something strange is going on, it's not like them to be so active in such a small area. It's like they're after something."

Autumn noticed Zilzina appraising her out of the corner of her eye. "How am I supposed to know?" she shrugged. The demon's scent was growing closer. "Behind us."

"No," Zilzina said, pausing for a moment before grabbing Autumn and leaping backward. "Above."

The devil slammed into the ground where they had just been, its claws and fangs finding nothing but air. Everything felt like it was moving in slow motion. Zilzina fired her pistol mid-air, striking the demon's head dead-center. Autumn hadn't even seen her draw the three-barreled weapon. Her skill with it was impressive. By the time Zilzina and Autumn landed, the fiend lay crumpled in the snow, dead.

"Wow," Autumn exclaimed, catching her breath. "I thought for sure it was behind us."

Zilzina holstered her gun and kicked the corpse to ensure it wouldn't be getting back up. "You mixed up its current and residual scents."

"Oh," Autumn said. She really did have a lot to learn. "How did you know?"

"My sense of smell is probably nowhere near yours, but I've trained for years to handle attacks like these. You have to pay attention to the scent's movements over time."

"Does it have a bounty on it?" the girl asked. She looked at the demon's face as they passed. It was twisted in rage with a still smoking hole blown straight through one of its eyes.

"Unlikely. The people of a village like this don't have the money to put out a real bounty."

"Right." Autumn paused. "Are you going to…"

"No," Zilzina replied shortly, though her eyes were flaring up a bit.

Autumn immediately regretted the question. Whether or not Zilzina needed to feed was her business, no one else's. "Sorry."

"It's fine," the elf said and picked up the pace. "Come on, we're almost there."

It was late afternoon by the time they finally approached the village. Zilzina pulled her hood up and told Autumn to do the same. The girl could understand how her dusky red scales and horns would be a problem, but she didn't think anyone would be more than awestruck by Zilzina's stark demeanor. Perhaps the elf just didn't like the attention.

The village was a conglomerate of low houses beside a small market. Autumn had been here once before, only briefly, when her mother had bought supplies and learned what she could of the surrounding areas. The people here were mostly oni and orcs. For all its allusions to integration and acceptance, Frigia was a highly segregated realm. Oni and orcs specifically suffered from intense racial prejudices, namely for the onis' demonic past–ancient history at this point–and the orcs' natural aggression. Villages like this with high concentrations of the non-human races were therefore common; the humans generally kept more to themselves, though some places, like Sapoul, were a melting pot of the different peoples of Frigia.

"Do you know where we're going?" Autumn asked as they entered the market.

"Yes," Zilzina replied. "I was here for a while before I found you."

They walked straight ahead toward the meeting hall. The village was rural, not even sporting tarred roads or electric streetlamps. There were no factories or motor vehicles. Even generators were rare here despite their commonness in the inner towns.

Zilzina walked up to the meeting hall door and knocked loudly. The building had seen better days but sported an oni mural depicting some battle Autumn didn't recognize, not that she was in the state of mind to care at the moment.

"I really don't want to be here, Zilzina," Autumn pleaded. "Take me with you. Please!"

Sympathy flashed across the hunter's eyes. Autumn dared to hope that she'd made her case, but her hopes were quickly dashed. "Come on," Zilzina mumbled, pushing inside as the building's large doors swung open.

Autumn followed reluctantly.

There was no one near the doors within. In fact, no one could be seen at all, though Autumn was sure she could smell several beings amidst the dusty pews. Gray sunlight filtered in through dirty stained-glass windows above a raised dais at the other end. Oni battle masks and orcish ritual weapons lined the walls.

"What is this place?" Autumn asked. She sniffed and sneezed at the dust, sending several sparks skittering out over the wooden floors.

"Careful," Zilzina warned. "It's where the village chief addresses the town."

"Why is it so musty?"

"Don't ask me," Zilzina shrugged.

Just then an elderly oni stepped out from a passageway near the dais. Night black hair and eyes set a stark contrast against her bright red skin. Horns protruded from the hair, not unlike Autumn's, though these were much larger, and a set of tusks grew from the mouth.

"I've come to speak with the chief," Zilzina said to the newcomer. She gestured to Autumn. "I slew a demon in the forest, but this girl's home was destroyed. She needs a place to live."

Autumn could feel the age in the old woman's voice as she

spoke. "The chief sends his apologies," she said with a slight lisp, stepping forward on the dais and outstretching a hand. "And who is this girl whom you have brought us and whose blood smells of fire?"

What did she mean, blood that smells like fire? Autumn glanced at Zilzina. The elf lowered her hood and motioned for Autumn to do the same.

The oni frowned. "Horns and scales," she whispered though it rang clearly in the musky air.

"She is a cambion," Zilzina said. "Her mother was a human and the father a demon. Both are now dead." She paused and looked back at Autumn before continuing. "I implore you to take her into your care. As a hunter, I can assure you that she is no threat."

Autumn could feel her chest tightening.

"The name cambion should never have existed," the female oni spat. "A half demon is still a demon. A lesser devil is still a demon. Even a human is still a demon."

What does she mean by humans being demons? Autumn wondered. She saw Zilzina tense and prepared herself to move. Something was about to happen.

"Where is the chief?" Zilzina's features settled into a scowl.

"Unavailable," the oni replied dismissively. She gestured and two more oni and an orc stepped out from the shadowy corners.

Had they been there the whole time? Autumn hadn't even sensed them. The oni were wearing their traditional face masks, red ceramic molded into a demonic face with large horns and fanged teeth. The orc bore a design in red face paint. Even its large tusks, protruding from the mouth, were painted.

"We're leaving," Zilzina said and turned. The doors slammed shut though no one was there.

"I thank you for bringing the girl to us," the female oni continued, donning her own mask, a white ceramic face crisscrossed with dark streaks. "We will do her the favor of ending her life before she becomes a real threat."

"She's under my protection," replied Zilzina coldly.

"No matter. You are an abomination yourself. We will do you both the favor."

"Autumn," Zilzina said without turning to her. Her voice was low enough that only they could hear. "Our goal is to escape. If I kill any of them, forget that the village is poor, there will be a price on our heads."

"Okay," Autumn replied. "I underst-"

Everything felt slow as the female oni seemed to disappear before their eyes. Where she had been just a second before it was as if a ghostly image of her remained, an afterimage due to incredible speed. She was actually beside Autumn, lashing out with a thin, curved sword. The girl wouldn't be able to get out of the way in time.

Zilzina was faster though. She shoved Autumn out of the way and swept the oni's feet out from under her in one deft movement. It was a good thing the villagers couldn't afford guns, she mused, or else they'd have been shot by now. More importantly, however, were the oni's movements. Some sort of magic was allowing her to displace herself at a moment's notice.

Autumn stumbled backward and ducked a lunging grab from the orc. She noticed the female oni's strange ethereal movements as she seemed to blink around Zilzina. Anyone else would've been long dead by then but the elf was fast. She parried and dodged in a blur of silver clashing with steel. Obviously, the oni was a sorceress of some kind; not unheard of, but Autumn was awestruck just the same.

Zilzina pushed back the female oni and rolled to defend Autumn as the other oni and orc approached. "Get out of here," she hissed to the girl. "Don't worry about me."

The sorceress was chanting a spell now, arms outstretched and circling in an ethereal motion, leaving ghost images as her movements had before. Autumn spun around and made for the exit only a moment too late. One of the other oni grabbed her dress and yanked her back.

"Heh," the orc huffed, stepping toward her, and raising his battle axe. Its tusks, covered in the same red paint as its face, were rather long and thick, an indicator of age and experience.

"Let me go!" Autumn demanded. She pushed back with all her might, knocking the oni who held her off balance and avoiding the orc's swing. The cambion girl looked to Zilzina but realized the hunter was engaged with the other oni warrior and the sorceress. Having seen the elf fight before, Autumn could tell Zilzina was holding back.

With a last shouted phrase, the oni sorceress brought a cacophony of sound Autumn hadn't noticed until then to a climax. A barrage of sharp icicles shot in Zilzina's direction. She spun, kicking the oni warrior aside and withdrew the whip from its holster at her hip. With a practiced ease, she spun it in a circle, its runes glowing bright orange and the light extending down along the entire weapon to create a golden aura.

Autumn realized she was creating a shield. Luckily the splinters of ice deflected off it and knocked her assailants off balance. Things were looking up for now but how long could the elf keep this up? The oni sorceress showed no signs of stopping.

"I would have expected your kind to understand… how it feels to be judged by your nature and not your actions," Zilzina grunted, obviously straining to keep up her shield.

"Do not lecture me, elf," the oni laughed, letting up the

barrage.

"Zilzina, look out!" Autumn screamed. Both the oni warrior and the orc had turned and were rushing her now that the ice barrage had let up. Digging her heel into her captor's foot, Autumn dropped and managed to wrest herself free of the other oni's grip.

Faced with two surprise assailants, Zilzina did her best to parry and dodge but there was only so much she could do. Knocking the orc's axe aside, she tried to sidestep a thrust from the oni warrior's sword but was a split second too late. It slipped easily into her side, a dark stain spreading from the wound.

"Zilzina!" Autumn screamed. She leapt forward, blood boiling and steaming tears rolling from her eyes. The fire was rising inside her, she could feel it. Several of the nearest pews burst into flame and the sorceress' eyes went wide in terror.

"Stop her!" the oni woman screamed as a gust of hot air buffeted her back, away from Autumn.

A sudden pain and coldness were all that Autumn remembered as her vision suddenly started fading to black. Something had hit her hard from behind. *Zilzina... was this my fault?* It didn't really matter...

In the last moment before she passed out, Autumn saw Zilzina lift herself shakily off the ground and unroll her sleeve. The pale arm beneath was laced with wicked looking tattooed designs. As she reached out toward the sorceress, the tattoos started to glow. Zilzina's face was twisted in rage.

Autumn felt that same cold fear as she had on that night when she'd come across the elf feeding.

"Dark magic," the oni sorceress whispered as Autumn lost consciousness. The oni's voice was heavy in the musty air.

CHAPTER III

Zilzina stumbled. She was weak, in pain. She needed to feed again to heal her wounds.

Autumn was fading in and out of consciousness, draped over the elf's shoulder. She saw the village disappearing behind them as evening came on. How long they walked she didn't know. Once or twice, she thought she saw shadows of pursuers on the horizon behind them, but no one ever approached. The pair stumbled onward, not knowing where they were going. The relative safety of the forest was long behind them–Zilzina had made a wrong turn somewhere but there was no doubling back now.

"What are you doing out here?" someone asked from ahead. Autumn tried to turn but couldn't see over Zilzina's shoulder. The hunter shifted to give her a better view.

On the road ahead a dwarf child and woman, perhaps his

mother, eyed the haggard pair suspiciously–or rather, the child eyed them. The mother seemed rather aloof. Behind them lay a sled with a dead deer on it.

"Who's there Klaus?" the woman asked. Her sightless eyes scanned the area reflexively. Were she not blind, she would've seen an injured Zilzina, blood soaking her clothing and a wild look in her eyes, carrying a cambion girl, scales and horns in full view.

"Mother," the child called as he approached them. "There are two girls who need our help."

***

Zilzina was sitting on a chair in the corner, facing the door. Autumn lay unconscious on the bed beside her.

"I'm sorry Autumn," the hunter whispered. It had been naive of her to think the oni would be sympathetic to the cambion's plight. Ancient connection or not, they were as fearful of demons as anyone else. They had every reason to despise those creatures that posed a constant threat to them. Even then, she had thought they would at least hear her out. Could she really blame them though? After all, she had drawn her pistol on Autumn when they first met.

Zilzina sighed. She'd gone too far in dealing with their attackers in the village. The rage she'd felt when they'd attacked Autumn, who was just a girl even if she was half demon, that anger still burned though she knew there was no point to it.

They were all dead now. Killed with black magic, burned alive from the inside out with darkflame.

Other villagers had certainly seen her and Autumn enter the building. Even more were likely to have seen them leave, hobbling out as the orc and oni screamed inside. *Shit.* There would be a price on her head for sure now. She couldn't afford to let her guard down, though her vision was blurring from pain and lack of sleep.

Beside her Autumn stretched and rubbed at her eyes, then sprang upright. "W- what's going on?" the girl asked. "Where are we?"

"Your ability to heal is impressive," Zilzina said, her breathing uneven. "Many others might have died from a blow like that."

Autumn's eyes went wide when she saw the blood on Zilzina's clothes. "What about you? Let me see!" She stood up quickly and helped the elf over into the bed. "Ok, easy. Let me see."

Zilzina gritted her teeth and pulled back her cloak, revealing a wound in her abdomen that had been hastily bound with a torn cloth.

"Ok, we need to get these off," Autumn said, starting to untie the cloth. "I need to clean and stitch the wound."

Zilzina grabbed her hand firmly. "Do you know what

you're doing?"

"Yes, my mom taught me." Autumn met the intense gaze of the elf's glowing eyes calmly.

Zilzina considered for a moment then let go. "Okay. There's a sewing kit in my pack."

Autumn was rummaging through the small pack as Zilzina stripped off her outerwear with some difficulty when a knock sounded at the door.

"Who's that?" Autumn hissed, spinning around with the stitching kit in hand. She realized she had no idea whose house they were even in.

"It's okay, let them in," Zilzina managed.

Autumn nodded and approached the door, unlocking it and opening it slightly. On the other side, a dwarf stood. His bright blue eyes and short cropped beard betrayed his age— dwarves' facial hair began growing at an early age, even among the women. He was carrying a bowl of steaming water and several cloths. "For your sister," he said. His gaze drifted past Autumn to the elf propped up in the small bed, prompting him to look down quickly with a mild flush. She still wore her underclothes, now stained with blood, but he didn't feel right staring all the same. "I'll bring food next," he continued. Autumn nodded, taking the bowl and cloths before he shuffled off.

"What happened?" Autumn asked as she returned and

knelt to begin cleaning the wound.

"They, ah-" the hunter flinched. "They decided to help us. Gods know why."

"Well, good thing they did. You wouldn't have gotten far like this." Autumn finished cleaning the area and threaded the needle. "Alright, deep breath."

"Just do it."

It wasn't the neatest stitching Zilzina had ever seen but she was grateful. This girl knew a lot for someone who had been hidden away from the world her entire life. She shifted uncomfortably as Autumn was finishing and tying off the thread. A few steaming teardrops fell onto her abdomen.

"Autumn…" the hunter said, putting a hand on the girl's shoulder.

Autumn turned away and wiped her eyes. "I thought you were going to die. And it would've been my fault. I know you'll say it wasn't, but they only attacked us because of me," she said with a sniff. "I didn't want to be alone. You're all I have, okay? Even if we did just meet. You can't die, do you hear me?" On that last word she turned back and met Zilina's gaze.

It was an outrageous request, but Zilzina couldn't help but smile a bit. "I hear you. And it isn't your fault. If I hadn't tried to-"

"None of this would've happened if you'd never met me,"

Autumn cut her off.

They were quiet for a while before Zilzina spoke again. "I'll take you to my home. You'll be safe there, I promise."

"Okay," Autumn sighed. "Though maybe we could try laying low for a while first."

"No arguments here," the elf whispered as she drifted off to sleep.

Autumn pulled the sheets up over her and took the chair to stand guard. By the time the dwarf boy returned with food, they were both sound asleep.

***

The next morning Zilzina and Autumn were halfway through their third helpings of deer soup, delivered dutifully in rounds by the dwarf boy, whose name they learned was Klaus. It was day, though they kept the windows shuttered. Overhead a lightbulb flickered merrily.

"They have a generator way out here, isn't that a little weird?" Autumn asked.

"A bit, though the dwarves are known for their technical skills," Zilzina replied between mouthfuls of soup. "And honestly I'm more grateful than worried."

"True," Autumn said, digging into her own soup. Several mouthfuls later she piped up cheerfully, "I've never met a dwarf. He's really short."

"Dwarves don't like being called short," Zilzina warned.

She finished her bowl and laid back on the bed.

Blood. Blood. Blood. She needed to feed soon. It didn't matter what food she ate when it got like this, she was insatiate until she'd had her fill of fresh demon's blood. She'd tried keeping extra in a skin before, but it seemed to lose its effect quickly after the host died. And it certainly didn't help that Autumn was around. Zilzina could feel her cravings intensify whenever she moved closer. There was something about her blood. She'd noticed it when the cambion had cut herself while preparing the rabbit and later when the oni sorceress had mentioned the fire in her blood. That was an apt description. Autumn's blood smelled like fire. Zilzina couldn't help but wonder what it tasted like…

"Oh, do you need to, you know?" Autumn asked, walking over and hovering over the bed. Her dark hair hung down and swung lazily, wafting the scent of her blood everywhere.

"Stop," Zilzina grunted. She could feel the veins starting to stand out in her neck.

"Right, sorry," Autumn replied, stepping back quickly.

Zilzina didn't answer. At the moment she really couldn't.

"I just noticed that you're still-"

"Autumn, it's fine," managed the hunter.

Autumn hushed and settled back into the chair.

Zilzina sighed. She hadn't meant to sound so harsh. "I know you still have questions," she said at last. "Ask them before I change-"

"What are those tattoos on your hand?" The words were out of Autumn's mouth before Zilzina had even finished speaking.

Zilzina glanced down at her arm. It was entirely covered in wicked looking arcane designs. She rarely allowed them to be exposed. "These are spells. I only use them in emergencies."

"Like back at the village? Is it dark magic?"

"Yes, they're dark magic and shouldn't be used unless absolutely necessary."

"Wow," murmured Autumn. She was examining the designs from her spot in the corner. Magic was rare and she'd never heard of anything like this before. Zilzina shifted so she could see better.

"Did you learn it yourself?"

"No," Zilzina said. She sat up, gritting her teeth in pain. "I'm just a medium."

"Careful." Autumn tried to help but the hunter waved her off.

Zilzina reached under the bed and brought out her whip, handing it to Autumn. The girl examined the runes in the handle.

"Someone very close to me gave me this and the tattoos," Zilzina said, her voice drifting off into memory. "She wanted to protect me since I insisted on hunting demons." The elf scoffed. "Maybe she was right. Maybe I should have stayed."

"She sounds amazing," Autumn mused.

"Yeah, she is. I'm sure you'll hear all about it when we get there."

"Oh. That's where you're taking me? Is she your mother?"

"Sort of. Her name is Serah."

Somehow the impressed look on Autumn's face made Zilzina feel proud. Her mother was pretty amazing.

"So... what happened to your real parents? Your birth parents I mean."

Zilzina took the whip back and coiled it slowly. "The demon Sannazu killed them. That's when he cursed me. We were travelers, my father was an acrobat at fairs across Frigia and my mother sold jewelry. Our caravan happened across him on the road. He killed everyone. Everyone but me."

"I'm sorry," Autumn replied solemnly. "Why do you think he let you live?"

"I don't know. Maybe it was on a whim. A sick joke." Zilzina's tone was cold, but she continued. "After that I wandered for a good while, begging for help. Because of how sickly the curse had made me look, people were scared. No one would help. That's when I met Serah." Autumn heard the elf's tone soften slightly. "*Young girl*, she said when she saw me, *come along and help me with these bags*. For some reason I did. From then on, she was like a mother to me. She lives in

Sapoul, taking care of people like me. Like us."

"Cursed?"

"Outcasts. The people no one else will accept."

"That sounds wonderful," Autumn said, a happy knot forming in her throat.

"It is. We have a long way to go."

"Alright, let's get you better first!" Autumn's voice rose in excitement. "I can't wait."

"Not so loud," Zilzina laughed. "We're guests, remember?"

"Right, sorry. You know, maybe we should thank our hosts."

"Later," the elf murmured as she drifted back toward sleep. "Just need to rest a bit..."

***

Zilzina woke up with a start. It was more like she had fallen unconscious than going to sleep. Autumn was snoozing on the chair in a position that must have been uncomfortable. She'd tried to convince the girl to share the bed with her, but Autumn insisted that it was better for Zilzina to have as much space as she needed.

The elf checked her wound. It was already healing, but slowly. Elves and demons both recovered at accelerated rates, though the latter had much stronger healing abilities. Autumn herself was evidence of that, already totally recovered from a blow to the back of the head that would have killed most people.

Sitting up carefully, Zilzina winced. She could accelerate her healing if she were to feed, but she was in no shape to hunt. And she didn't dare risk accepting Autumn's help. Not for something so dangerous. She stood and picked up Autumn gingerly, laying her on the bed. The girl writhed a bit uncomfortably and murmured "leave me alone."

"So stubborn," Zilzina whispered and shook her head with a smirk. She left the room quietly, hating that she found herself wishing that a devil was around. The harsh reality was she needed one, and soon.

Sannazu. If only she could find the bastard who'd cursed her.

"Oh, who's there? Klaus?" the dwarf woman called out from her rocking chair in the main room. She was threading beads together. Zilzina had noticed a number of bead artworks in their room and the hall.

A blind artist. Amazing.

"Uh, no. My name is Zilzina," the elf replied. She wasn't used to accepting help from strangers, not since she'd left Serah.

"Ah, you must be one of the girls my little Klaus found. Is your sister with you?"

"No, she's still sleeping."

"All is well then," she said, setting her beadwork on the

stool beside her. "Come here child, let me hold your hand."

It was a strange request, but Zilzina thought better than to deny it. They had given her and Autumn a safe place to rest after all. She walked over and offered her hand. The woman took it, her own small hands worn and calloused with age.

"Oh my," she exclaimed, rubbing a thumb across the back of Zilzina's hand. "What a powerful elf you are. Strange though... so cold."

"Did your son tell you I'm an elf?" Zilzina asked.

"Oh no," the woman replied. She let go of Zilzina's arm and picked up her beadwork again. "Klaus is only twenty-nine but he's a good boy. He tries to shelter me from the world. It was his idea to bring you in, you know, and he's been taking care of everything."

"I see," Zilzina said, immediately regretting the word choice. "How did you know?"

"There are more ways to see than meets the eye." The woman smiled to herself. "Enough about me though. I'm sure you have some things to do. Klaus is out hunting in the forest if you'd like to give him a hand."

"Yes, um, thank you," said the elf. "For taking us in I mean. We'll leave as soon as we can."

"No rush, dear," the dwarf replied. "It's just me and Klaus all the time. A little company is always nice. And it's Martha, by the way."

"Martha, right. Thank you." She'd spent too much time hunting demons–the hunter's social graces were in a poor state. All the same, she meant it. She was thankful for the risk Martha and Klaus were taking. Kindness to strangers was a rare thing in Frigia, especially given her and Autumn's unique situation.

It took some time for Zilzina to reach the forest proper. Maratha's house was in a depression at the bottom of a fairly steep incline, which led to deep snowdrifts. Once there, she found Klaus easily. He was a short way inside the wood, crouching behind a tree. He didn't seem to notice as Zilzina approached. She was curious to see what he was doing and remained silent.

Klaus shifted in anticipation as a rabbit hopped into a small clearing a little ahead of him. It sniffed the air and began to tread careful. In the center of the clearing was an obvious trap, a piece of carrot set in the middle of a small rope loop, only suddenly it wasn't. Klaus waved his hand and the trap turned into a patch of vegetation before Zilzina's eyes.

"Illusion magic," Zilzina whispered just a little too loudly. Klaus was startled and the vegetation faded, sending the rabbit bounding off in fear. "Sorry," Zilzina said to the now dejected looking young dwarf.

"Well, there goes breakfast," he mused, standing and brushing off his knees.

"You use illusion magic," Zilzina said again.

Klaus didn't bother turning to her. He walked over and gathered up his trap. "Yes, I do," he answered.

"Who taught it to you?"

"I learned it from some books my mother has."

Self-taught? At his age? "That's amazing," was all she could think to say.

He turned back to her, a slight smile on his face. "Only a rare person like you would think so."

True. Many would view the use of illusion magic, often called fey trickery, with suspicion. "Why do you and your mother live so far out here alone?" Zilzina continued as they walked along through the forest looking for more prey. She shortened her strides appropriately, so she didn't outpace the dwarf.

"My father found the outside world... irritating, so he built us a house out here when I was little," Klaus said. There was a somber note in his tone. "He died a few years later of a strange illness, the same illness that left my mother blind."

"I'm sorry," Zilzina said.

"Don't be. It won't help."

Klaus was an interesting kid, that was certain. For a dwarf, he was remarkably young yet still took on enormous responsibility for his mother. Zilzina was impressed.

"Do you hunt for most of your food?" she asked after a

while.

"For the meat, yes," Klaus replied. "I go to the market twice a month with my mother for other things."

"Where do you get the coins?"

"Money has never been a problem," Klaus said confidently, flipping a silver coin in the air from nowhere. It disappeared in the next instant as he made a dramatic flourish.

Well then, perhaps a little of the suspicion toward illusion magic was warranted. "You're doing great, kid," she said and ruffled his hair.

Klaus made no answer, just blushed a bit and quickened his pace. A short while later, Zilzina broke off in a separate direction.

"Where are you going?" the dwarf asked.

"There's something I need to do," she answered. "I'll return to the house soon."

"Can you find your way back?"

Zilzina just grinned and waved him off as she continued her trek. Once she was far enough away, the hunter unsheathed her silver dagger and drew a thin line of blood on her left forearm. Any demon in the surrounding area would smell the blood. She hoped there was one close enough.

***

It was night by the time Zilzina returned to the dwarves' home. Klaus, Martha, and Autumn sat at an outdoor table with a small fire nearby, all engaged in beadwork projects. Autumn had created a crude image of her cabin, the one that had burned those several nights before.

Autumn was in the midst of a telling story that was probably best kept secret. She wore only her dress, the bulky overcoat that hid her nature nowhere to be seen. *She really never gets cold.* Zilzina simply shook her head and let the ridiculous girl continue.

"...and then this huge orc with horns coming out of his mouth..." she continued excitedly as she slipped more beads onto the pattern she was making.

"Tusks," Klaus corrected.

"Yeah, whatever," Autumn went on without looking up. "Anyway, he hit me so hard I flew across the room–Zilzina!" She dropped her beadwork and ran across to the returning elf.

"Hey there," Zilzina said, more pleased to see her than she wanted to admit.

"You were gone the whole day," the girl admonished with a dramatic gesture.

"I know, it was important."

Autumn noted a dark spot on Zilzina's shirt. "Oh, right."

The elf walked over to the table and set down a pouch. "I found some mulberries. I hope you like them."

"As a matter of fact, I do," the elderly dwarf beamed.

Zilzina nodded to both Klaus and Martha–the latter

somehow knew to nod in return–and ducked through the front door. Making her way into the room she and Autumn were sharing, the hunter stood for a moment in silence, taking it all in. A wave of nausea overtook her and she ran to the window, pushing it open just as the bile rose in her throat. Not uncommon after feeding.

This went on for several minutes, drawing tears to Zilzina's eyes for the first time in a long while. She heard timid footsteps in the hall.

"You give it to her," Autumn whispered a little too loudly.

"Why do I have to give it to her while she's in a bad mood?" Klaus asked.

"Because you look like you're always in a bad mood too."

Klaus sighed and Zilzina saw the handle begin to turn.

"Try to cheer her up," Autumn continued. The handle stopped moving.

"Do I look like I can do that?"

"Just try, pleeease."

Zilzina wiped her face as Klaus finally pushed the door open and stepped into the room. He took a look at her and set down the mug he was holding on the side table. "Some wine my father left behind," he said soberly as he sat down in the nearby chair. "My mother wouldn't let me have any."

"Thanks," Zilzina said. She took a sip–it wasn't bad, a little bitter for her taste.

"Do you need anything else?"

The elf sat down on the bed, head bowed. "No, just a little time."

Klaus nodded and stood to leave, then seemed to think better of it, walked over to Zilzina and ruffled her silver hair. "You're doing great," he repeated in his best imitation of Zilzina's bored tone.

She laughed and wiped at her eyes again. *Damnit*, she wasn't supposed to cry.

***

The next morning Zilzina was up early. It seemed like Klaus went out hunting about this time. She had decided the night before to join him today. It was the least she could do after scaring off the rabbit the day before. And for everything else. She and Autumn would be on their way to Sapoul tomorrow.

They would see Serah soon. They would see her family.

The young cambion, who had just been snoring softly on the bed, rolled over lazily. "Hmm, what are you doing?"

"I'm going to help Klaus hunt for today," the elf replied.

"Oh…" Autumn stretched and rolled sleepily onto her feet. She set about putting her hair in a bun and looked around for her dress.

"What do you think you're doing?" Zilzina asked bemusedly.

"I'm going too," the girl replied. "There's nothing to do

here anyway."

"You? This early? I'm impressed."

Autumn simply stuck her tongue out and continued getting ready.

Zilzina reached under the bed and retrieved her enchanted whip, hanging it on her belt. The pistol and dagger followed soon after. She did a count and made a mental note to restock on silver bullets the next chance she had. They weren't rare, per se, but could be hard to find outside of the cities.

"Do you always carry all your weapons?" Autumn asked as they left the room.

"Yes."

"Don't you ever relax?"

"No."

"Why?" Autumn continued the questioning. They stepped outside, steam rising from the cambions dusky scales as it always did when she first went out into the cold.

"In case you bleed."

"What does that mean?"

Zilzina shrugged and looked around for Klaus. She spotted him with a large sack–at least for him–on the side of the house. There was something strange about Autumn's blood, but she wasn't sure what it was yet. Heck, there was something strange about Autumn.

"Oh, you're both awake," Klaus said as they approached.

"Are you going somewhere?"

"We're coming with you!" Autumn replied cheerfully.

"I don't need your help. I do this alone all the time," replied Klaus, shouldering his bag.

"It's hard to watch while being housed and fed for free," Zilzina said. She walked ahead of the dwarf, making a concerted effort to clear the path a bit for Klaus. Autumn trailed behind them.

Klaus sighed and shook his head but said nothing else.

"What do you plan on catching today?" Autumn asked once they were a short way into the woods.

"Deer," the dwarf replied.

"Eh... why is it always meat?" the girl asked.

Zilzina scooped up a handful of snow and flicked it toward her in reproach. Most of it missed but Autumn stuck out her tongue and leered all the same.

The fourteen-year-old girl was more childish than the dwarf. Granted, Klaus was in his late twenties but that was equivalent to ten or eleven in human years.

"We could hunt for fish if you like," Zilzina said. "Then you wouldn't have to deal with this one all day." She emphasized the words this one with a head nod toward Autumn.

"I don't know of any streams or ponds around that wouldn't be iced over this time of year," replied Klaus as

Autumn picked up her own handful of snow to fling.

"There's one west of here, down in one of the valleys." Zilzina and Autumn were circling carefully around Klaus now, the cambion threatening with a tightly packed snowball that was already melting at her touch. "I saw it yesterday. We'll be back in a few hours."

"I've never gone that far," Klaus said. He was completely ignoring the snow fight that was happening around and over him. "If you could show me where it is I could bring fish home for my mother after you leave, she'd like that. Plus, you two probably scared all the animals away already."

"Alright then, let's go," the hunter said. She sidestepped a snowball from Autumn and set off at a quick–but not too quick–pace toward the west.

***

The hot spring was located in a small valley and protected by a wide overhang.

Zilzina stripped down to her underclothes and stepped in. Autumn put her hand to cover Klaus' eyes although he had already looked away. They didn't have any fishing equipment, but the elf was fast enough to snag them with her bare hands. Several hours later Klaus was shouldering his bag again, now laden with fish, and Zilzina was shivering as Autumn rubbed her shoulders.

"You should have let me go in," the cambion said. "I don't

get cold, remember?'

"Yes, I remember," Zilzina said through chattering teeth as she pulled her boots back on and stood to leave. "I just thought it might be nice to catch something."

"I might, I used to hunt with my mom!" argued the girl.

"Fine, next time."

"Honestly, if I didn't know better, I'd think you were starting to get protective," the girl continued.

"Mhm," the elf replied with a heavy tone of sarcasm.

The trek back was uneventful. Klaus was paying special attention and making mental notes of the path the whole way. As they drew nearer to the house, Klaus suddenly stopped.

"Footprints," he whispered, pointing off to their right.

"I don't see anyth-" Autumn started when Zilzina cut her off.

"Is it a problem?" Zilzina's sharp eyes saw them immediately.

"No one ever comes out here. I don't know."

They approached carefully, circling around behind a small hill to stay hidden from view. They crested carefully and crouched as the house came into view. Martha stood out front surrounded by several bulky orcs and a sword-wielding oni. Autumn gasped and Zilzina cursed, shoving both the cambion and dwarf to the ground as she dropped to her stomach.

Autumn's face said it all. They'd been followed. Her mouth opened but closed quickly again when Zilzina shook her head in warning.

Klaus crawled up to look over the edge of the hill again. "You both wait here and don't come out," he said. "I have to go help my mother." He rose and trudged off toward the gathering. Zilzina considered stopping him but decided against it

The cambion and hunter edged up to watch as Klaus approached his mother and the visitors. They couldn't hear well due to the wind, but their voices drifted intermittently in the hill's direction.

"What's going on?" Autumn whispered.

"Hush," hissed the elf.

"Who are you? Why are you keeping my mother out in the cold?" Klaus called as he approached the house.

"Son, is that you? Come here," Martha said. Her voice was laced with a cheerfulness in stark contrast with the situation. The orcs and oni sneered but let Klaus pass without issue. The boy took his mother's hand and turned to face the group gathered in front of their house.

"These people seem to be looking for something," Martha continued.

"The house is covered with their scent," spat one of the orcs.

"Where are they," asked the oni. Its deep voice cut through the air.

"Where are who?" Klaus asked innocently.

"Do not play dumb with me," the same orc said, stepping forward threateningly.

Klaus stepped confidently forward in front of his mother. "Oh, you mean the elf and the demon girl? They're over there, making a run for it."

Right before their eyes Zilzina and Autumn saw copies of themselves appear, running away from the house and away from them.

"What the...?" Autumn murmured.

"Illusion magic," Zilzina explained. She was impressed–this was much bigger than creating a patch of vegetables. Klaus was seriously talented.

"Oh, wow."

The orcs and oni immediately sprinted after the illusions with shouts of "there they are" and "get them!"

The fake Zilzina turned back and shouted, "run Autumn!" before charging the attackers. They cut the illusion down easily, leaving a bloody corpse. Fake or not it was unnerving to see oneself cut down like that.

"Zilzina!" the illusory Autumn cried, turning to run back.

The attackers didn't hesitate. She toppled to the ground in a puff of snow. It was gut wrenching but better than seeing the real thing.

"These are the ones who killed Elder Kala? How pitiful," the orc roared.

Martha was saying something to Klaus, and he took her hand. Zilzina could've sworn she looked up toward her and Autumn. She could've sworn a sad smile flashed across the old dwarf's face.

"They have a generator so there must be fuel," the orc was shouting. He appeared to be in charge. "We'll burn the scum."

"Isn't that a bit unnecessary?" Martha asked mildly. Zilzina and Autumn could barely make out her words. "We can bury them."

"They didn't seem to think so when they did the same to my kind," the orc replied gruffly. His accomplices burst into the house and began ransacking it. They returned shortly with a large can, pouring it over the illusory corpses. The bodies may have been fake, but the fire certainly looked real as it flared up. The lead orc returned and dropped the can at Martha's feet with a thud.

"Well, we have a lot of work to do," Martha said. She reached out for Klaus. "I am sure you have a long journey back home."

"Woah, woah, what's the rush woman?" the orc asked. "Do you have a problem being among orcs and oni? Do we bother you?"

Martha shifted her gaze toward the head orc. "Of course not," she said. "May I hold your hand, dear?"

The orc chuckled and stretched out his large hand to hers. Martha took it gingerly.

"It is not your race that bothers me," she continued, bowing her head. "It is your heart."

"Heh." The orc withdrew a long knife from his belt.

"Run," Martha whispered. Zilzina felt it in her mind more than heard it, as if the woman was somehow sending the message to her as well as Klaus.

In a flash of red and silver, the orc slashed through Martha's neck, severing her head. Arterial spray flew in a crescent across the orc and Klaus as Martha's head rolled to the young dwarf's feat.

"Huh?" was all Klaus could say as he fell to his knees. He caressed Martha's hair gently. "Why- why would you... You already found who you were after..."

A primal roar rose up in the young dwarf's chest as the orc stepped forward to make another swing.

"Zilzina! We have to-"

"No," the elf replied coldly, pressing Autumn back down into the snow. "Don't let their sacrifice be in vain."

Autumn looked away as the blade came down. She didn't need to see another friend die tonight. Hot tears streamed down her face. She needed to scream but Zilzina pressed a hand firmly over her mouth. She couldn't move, she couldn't scream, she just wept.

"Stay still," the elf hissed. She could feel her own voice trembling in sorrow and rage. "Please stay still."

These thugs weren't strong. She could kill them easily. She could slaughter them all without a second thought. It would be easy. But then more would come, looking for her and Autumn. They can't have died for nothing. Sometimes the best revenge was living, something she had made peace with long ago.

You both wait here and don't come out. Klaus's last words to them. How had she been so stupid? Of course they wouldn't let them live. There would be problems if it were known they had hunted down and killed an elf, alleged criminal or not.

"Burn it all down," the orc leader was saying. The others dragged Klaus and Martha inside. Before long the entire house was aflame.

"We have to go," Zilzina said, pushing Autumn to leave. She saw the bright fire of another homestead dancing in the girl's eyes.

Autumn shook her head and kept watching. She wasn't thinking straight.

"Ok," the elf continued and hoisted the cambion up onto her shoulder. "Just breathe." She ran as fast she could into the forest, heedless of direction. What was important was that they get out of there.

Sometime later, once Autumn had found her legs and trailed along behind Zilzina, they stopped to rest. They hadn't exchanged a word in what seemed like hours. The moon was high overhead.

"Why didn't we help?" Autumn asked at last, her voice raw with anger. Zilzina felt her heart break just a little more with the silence. "We didn't... you didn't even try."

Zilzina stopped and turned to her. "You think I wanted them to die?" Her voice betrayed an irritation mixed with anger that she hadn't expressed to the girl before.

"Well, you should have let me go!"

"And what the fuck would you have done?" Zilzina shouted back. Everything came to a quiet standstill, the words echoing between them. Each heartbeat felt like hours.

"I... I don't know." Tears poured down Autumn's face, sizzling into the snow below. "I have no idea. But we- we did nothing and now they're dead!"

The cambion fell to her knees. They stayed like that for some minutes, the feeling of guilt and shame in Zilzina's stomach growing with each passing moment. Why had she shouted like that? She was mad at herself, not Autumn. She never realized how hard this was. Serah would've known what to do...

Zilzina kneeled and embraced the sobbing girl. "I'm sorry," she whispered. "I'm really sorry."

"They didn't do anything wrong." Autumn's voice was shaky. "Why would they…"

"The world is a cycle. A really shitty cycle of hatred and violence. I know that doesn't make you feel any better and it doesn't change anything but… that's the only explanation I have."

"I don't think I can understand."

Zilzina's grim face melted into a sad smile. "That's okay. I wish I didn't sometimes." After a pause, the elf stood again and offered Autumn her hand. "Come on, let's get moving. Sapoul is still a long way off."

As they set off again, Zilzina wondered if she had made the right choice. It didn't feel right. It felt selfish and stupid. Two of the best people in the world were dead because she failed to act. She should have killed those criminals, consequences be damned. But it was too late now. Now all that mattered was getting Autumn somewhere safe.

That's what Martha and Klaus had died for after all.

CHAPTER IV

"Zilzinaaaa," Autumn whined as she trailed behind the elf. She knew that her traveling companion couldn't withstand her complaints forever. "Zilzinaaaaaaaaaaaa!"

"Stop being childish, Autumn," the hunter replied in exasperation. The last week had been a long one indeed.

The cambion pouted in a manner overtly childish. "But I'm tired," she said.

"I already told you that we'll stop at the next village. It shouldn't be much farther"

"You said that this morning," Autumn continued whining. "It's almost evening now."

"Well, we're closer now than we were. Now come on," Zilzina said and trudged along. Truth be told, she was beginning to wear as well but she wouldn't let Autumn know that. The girl was impossible sometimes.

"You must be a devil," muttered Autumn just loud enough that she knew the elf could hear it. "Never getting tired."

"Oh hush. I said we were close earlier to get you to stop. And guess what? It didn't work. So now you know I'm telling the truth when I say that we are close."

"Ugh, we'll never get there."

"Yes, we will. Soon."

"Honestly, I'm not sure I can trust you anymore." Autumn twirled as she walked.

Zilzina took out her whip and spun the end of it idly at her side, creating a golden circle. "Looks like you have plenty of energy to me."

The girl stopped twirling and sighed. At least Zilzina was trying to entertain her, but it wasn't working. *It must be tough traveling with a child after so long on your own*, Autumn thought. She guessed that she was probably really annoying to the elf demon hunter but didn't care much at the moment.

"So how far away are we from Sapoul now?" Autumn asked. She scooped up a twig and flicked it into the twirling whip, sending a hundred glowing sparks off from the impact.

"Not far, several days beyond the next village," replied Zilzina. She reversed the direction of her whip's spin. "We're getting into respectable territory now so you're going to have to behave yourself."

"I always behave myself!"

"Mhm."

Autumn fell quiet as they walked along. She wanted to talk about Klaus and Martha but… they'd already talked about them so much in the past week. Zilzina never said anything, but the girl could tell that she didn't like the subject. Autumn didn't like it either but when they talked about it at least it felt like they weren't ignoring what happened. That's the least they could do, wasn't it?

In the end, she decided not to bring it up. Instead, she decided to chide Zilzina again–that was always fun at least. "I'm beginning to think you're unable to judge distance. Or time."

"How dare you?" the elf replied with a mock gasp. Autumn couldn't help but giggle a bit. "Maybe we aren't there yet because you keep saying that you're tired and that you want to take a break."

"I'm a growing girl." Autumn shrugged.

"If only you'd grow enough to stop whining." The tone was playful, but Zilzina half meant it. "We spent two nights in the last village because of you."

"They had strawberries!" cried Autumn. "Do you know how hard it is to-"

"Hood on, now," hissed the elf. Autumn pulled her cloak up without question. Two, no, three people were approaching them from down the road. They'd met a handful of travelers along the way, but they were becoming more frequent closer to Sapoul. As the others came into view, the cambion remembered to put her red, scaled hands in her pockets.

Three women, two elves and a human, approached them, laughing among themselves the whole way. They seemed absolutely carefree. Perhaps there were places in Frigia where people could live peacefully. Autumn thought back to the dwarves, Martha and Klaus, and how they'd treated them, before, well... And even the orcs and oni seemed to get along in their village. If only everyone could get along like that.

As the trio passed, one of the elven women, the one with brownish hair and a graceful stride, dropped a comb. She bent to pick it up and caught sight of Autumn's face. Their eyes met and the elven woman grimaced but simply hurried to catch up with her friends. They murmured and looked back at Zilzina and Autumn but went on without incident.

Zilzina exhaled with relief. "That was close-" she said before noticing that Autumn had stopped walking. "What's wrong?"

"I can't keep wearing this," replied the girl, flailing her worn out coat and dress. She assumed the most pitiful pleading face in her arsenal.

"Hm," Zilzina hummed and eyed the three women now disappearing into the distance behind them. They had been rather well dressed and altogether lovely. Not quite Zilzina's

74

thing but she understood where the girl was coming from. "I suppose you do need some gloves. And perhaps trousers would do better than a dress for travel."

"I want to look better, not like an assassin!" cried Autumn, thinking enviously back to the dresses of their passersby.

"Dresses aren't practical for travel anyway. Serah will make you one once we get there. Not to mention, I don't have much money."

"Have more shame when you say that," Autumn teased. "The greatest demon hunter in the land, broke."

Zilzina laughed. A real laugh, from the stomach, for the first time in a while. "There hasn't been much time to find bounties lately. But something will turn up, it always does."

"Maybe in the next village?"

"From the way those women were dressed, we can't be far now."

"That's what you said last time." Autumn knew she was right though. Before long, they were on the outskirts of a proper town, not like the hamlets and villages Autumn was familiar with. It was at the bottom of a gentle hill, giving Zilzina and Autumn a good view as they approached. Countless gaslights and bulbs winked out at them, highlighting the people bussing through the streets. As they got closer Autumn could see a wide variety of races–orcs, dwarves, elves, oni, and humans.

"I was here some months back," Zilzina said as they passed into the outer districts. "It's called Laguton, a trading post where goods from Sapoul are prepared to travel east or south along the major tradeways."

"Oooh," Autumn exclaimed, spotting a street vendor from which wafted the most delicious candy smell she had ever encountered.

Zilzina grabbed her collar and pulled her back. "Not so fast, we'll find somewhere to lay low and move around more freely after dark."

Autumn only agreed when the elf relented and spent one of their few remaining copper pieces on a pair of crystal candy sticks. Was it worth it? Probably not from a financial perspective, but sometimes the little things made a big difference. Zilzina hoped it would quiet the girl's complaints, at least temporarily.

***

It was a couple of hours before Zilzina thought it was dark enough to find lodgings. Autumn had whiled away the time by pestering her caretaker, as was her fashion. Unfortunately, the candy had done little to quell her moaning.

"Maybe we should've gone straight in," Zilzina sighed, standing up and stretching from her perch in the short alley. "Risked being found out."

"What's that supposed to mean?" Autumn feigned offense.

"Hood."

For the second time that day, Autumn flipped her cowl up quickly, drawing it low to cover her features.

"What do you want?" Zilzina called out.

A human woman approached slowly down the alley. Autumn cursed herself for not recognizing the scent or hearing her earlier. She needed to pay better attention in situations like these. Zilzina would definitely tell her so later.

"Wow, you really can't sneak up on a hunter, can you?" the woman said. She stepped into the moonlight, her green dress shimmering slightly.

"I'd advise you to stop trying," said Zilzina dryly. "Before someone mistakes you for a threat. And why do you think I'm a hunter?"

The woman laughed. "Noted, noted. And what else would you be, armed like that?"

An uncomfortable moment passed. "Why are you still here?" Zilzina broke the silence.

"Straight to the point, I like that," replied the woman uncomfortably. "I, uh, require your services. The agency wouldn't approve my request, but I'll pay." She lifted a heavy pouch from her belt. "I promise."

"I've heard that before," the hunter scoffed. "Payment up front."

"And I've heard that before. Hear me out and come with

me, and then I'll give you half if you agree to help."

A scowl etched its way over Zilzina's face. She'd had enough bad dealings to be suspicious of the woman, though she seemed genuine enough.

"We do need the money," Autumn whispered, tugging at Zilzina's elbow. "You said the right bounty would pop up."

"Yeah, I'm just not used to them literally popping up in the middle of the night," Zilzina whispered back. She thought for a moment and replied to the woman. "Okay, half up front."

"And I'll throw in room and board." The woman sounded relieved.

"What sort of demon are we talking about?" continued Zilzina, a little taken aback by the woman's generosity. This was certainly out of the ordinary in her line of work. Most people interacted with demon hunters as little as possible.

"I really don't know. A phantom by all accounts."

Zilzina sighed. "Okay, I'll help you. But first-" she rested a hand on Autumn's covered head "-this one needs some new clothes and a safe place to wait."

"And food," the cambion whispered.

"And food."

"Of course," the woman replied. "She is your...?"

"Pet," Zilzina muttered, earning a vicious foot stomp from Autumn. "Sister. My younger sister, her name is Autumn."

"Right, okay quickly." The woman turned and stalked purposefully out from the alley. "I know a boutique and then I'll take you to my home where you'll be housed and fed. And where the demon has struck, twice now."

The city streets were bright, even at night. The outskirts were mostly gas lamps, but the woman brought them to a nicer area where electric light bulbs lined the avenues. A motor carriage hobbled down the street past them, its exhaust pipes coughing out smoke in regular puffs.

"Z-Z-Zilzina," Autumn said absent mindedly, tugging the elf's elbow with each stutter. She watched the vehicle in awe

"You'll be seeing many more of those the closer we get to Sapoul," the elf responded, bemused. "Best get it out of your system now."

Zilzina had lived in a city for much of her life, though Serah had tried to keep her from wandering the streets. When she was very young, she spent much of her time in the window, watching motor carriages and crowds of people passing by. Once she was a little older, she would sneak out and eventually graduated to outright rebelliousness, dismissing Serah's warnings and doing as she pleased. Zilzina wished now to return to that time, when so few cares weighed upon her. When Serah had taken those cares for her and protected her.

Like she now cared for and protected Autumn. But Zilzina

wasn't made for that sort of thing. Her life was too dangerous. Serah would take the cambion on–she would know what to do. But now wasn't the time to be thinking about that.

In the glowing electric light Zilzina could see their benefactor's features better. The woman was middle aged, her slightly graying, auburn hair caught up in a loose bun.

"Did you ask her name?" Autumn said.

"Is that important?" replied Zilzina idly.

"How do I–a shut in–have better social skills than you?"

Oh, if only Autumn knew how many of Zilzina's years had been spent alone in her room. "Hey, lady," she called out. "What's your name?"

"Oh, how rude of me," the woman replied with a genuine sounding apology. "My name is Diona. And you are?"

"Zilzina."

"I'm Autumn," the cambion piped up, still holding on to Zilzina's elbow as they walked down the well-lit street.

"What lovely names." Diona really did sound genuine. "Ah, here we are."

They stopped in front of a wide storefront with what Zilzina thought was a sickening display of bright colors and floral designs in the window. As was her way, Autumn rushed inside with reckless abandon. The other two followed through the swinging door, three jingles of the doorbell in quick succession. The front counter appeared unattended, but a short step ladder peeked up over the edge.

"Hello?" Diona called. "I buy all my clothes here," she continued to Autumn and Zilzina, the former looking around in awe.

Autumn had never seen a store like this. Shelves upon shelves in neat aisles bearing all sorts of clothing she could have never even imagined.

"Just a moment," someone said from below the counter. The ladder shook as it was ascended and a dwarven man appeared shortly. "What can I help ya' with today?"

"Some clothes, breeches, and shirts. And gloves," Autumn piped up. "And a mask, if you have them."

"No masks I'm afraid," the dwarf replied. "Now if I could just-" he continued, reaching for her hood.

"She has a burn," Zilzina interjected as Autumn backed away quickly. "Prefers to keep the hood on."

"Oh, my apologies. Please have a look, you should find some things in your size down this way." The dwarf gestured toward the far side of the showroom. "And, of course, we can perform alterations as needed. A dressing room, just over there."

"I'll wait here," Diona said and turned to peruse some of the fancy affairs in the display window.

"Another close call," Zilzina whispered. "The mask is a good idea.

They picked through the aisle for clothing, coming up with two good sets of trousers, long sleeve shirts, underclothes, and gloves, as well as a new jacket and hooded coat. Autumn already sported a good set of boots. Leaving the girl to try everything on, Zilzina casually made her way toward a set of leather pants that had caught her eye, though she wouldn't admit it out loud.

Just as Autumn was trying on the last shirt, a thud sounded from outside the dressing room. She slipped into the new jacket and pulled the hood up before peeking out. There was no one there, just a pale mask with long dark hair attached to it on the floor. She picked it up carefully, still looking around for the owner. No one. The oni styled face of the mask was white and streaked with black lines, darker and thinner than those of the oni priestess who'd attacked them not so long ago. From the forehead extended extrusions for two small horns, and under the chin hung a thin, black cloth that would hide the neck when worn. The craftsmanship was exquisite.

It was a perfect make for Autumn.

"Do you like it?" a cool voice came from the aisle beside her.

Autumn gasped, jumping in fear and tripping backward into the dressing room. Her hood fell back, revealing her cambion nature to whomever the stranger was. A tall, dark-haired elven man stepped into view around the dressing room doorway. He smelled of flowers, a particularly alluring sort that the girl couldn't quite place, and wore a charming smile. His skin was pale–not quite as pale as Zilzina's but still noticeably–and his eyes were glowing red. Beautiful but fearful at the same time.

The only other person Autumn had ever seen with eyes like that was Zilzina, but she wasn't totally sure that it was uncommon. She hadn't met many elves in her life. Who was this man? He gave off an aura of... royalty?

"Do you like it?" he repeated, his voice like a wisp of sweet air.

"I, uh... who are you?" replied the girl.

"My name would be hard for you to say," he said and stretched out a hand to help her up. "But I work here as an aide."

"Oh, well, uh, thank you." The man's hand was quite cold, again not unlike Zilzina's.

"Well? Do you like the mask?"

"Right, yes. Thank you. I thought you didn't have any masks in. It's so..."

"Unique. I know." He turned to the shelves and began feeling the materials of the clothes. His eyes closed to a half-lidded state, reminiscent almost of euphoria. "It belonged to an oni long dead. Perhaps a thousand years now? Yes, that seems right. She was breathtaking. Whenever she wore this mask, the fates trembled."

"Wow, you speak as if you knew her," Autumn said breathlessly. The man's presence was somehow stifling.

He stopped feeling the fabrics and turned. "Ah, books can be quite descriptive. I am a great reader. And you?"

"Yes, I love to read," said the cambion girl. She didn't stop the man when he carefully brushed her hair back behind her ear.

"I think it will suit you nicely. Please, try it on." He gestured to the mirror within the fitting room.

Autumn turned to the mirror to put the mask on. She expected to see the man behind her, but no one was there. Double checking the aisle, the girl confirmed he had disappeared. Strange. She turned back to the mirror and fixed the mask to her face. It was perfect. So engrossed was she in her own reflection that she didn't see Zilzina approach and touch her shoulder.

"Hey, are you finished?" she asked, noticing the mask. "Wow, that's a nice piece."

"An aide dropped it off. He said something about a thousand-year-old oni, but it was probably just a story to get me to buy it," Autumn replied, though she secretly believed the tale. There was something, a feeling of power and antiquity, that washed over her when she donned the mask. "Anyway, yes, I'm ready." Noticing the leather breeches draped over Zilzina's arm the girl grinned. "Couldn't help yourself, could you? I saw you peeking at them."

"Well, mine are rather worn out. Plus, I can't let you have all the fun."

"True." Autumn gathered up all the clothes she had tried on. They were good fits, and they didn't have time to wait for tailoring anyway. "Okay, let's go."

"That mask is perfect though," Zilzina noted as they walked back to the counter. "Looks like it was made for you. Anyway, it should be easier to move around in public now–now people will only question your sanity and not your heritage."

"Because that's so much better." Autumn rolled her eyes. "What about you? I bet we could find you one to cover up those fangs and oh-so-pretty eyes."

"No thanks, hoods will suffice for me," replied the elf, pulling her cloak up for emphasis. Her features were strange but not so far out of the ordinary that they usually posed a threat. Still, she preferred not to draw attention.

When they reached the counter, Diona and the dwarf attendant, who had been chatting idly, both looked up in surprise at Autumn's mask.

"Wow," Diona said. "That looks, uh, great."

Eccentric and out of fashion was more like it but Autumn appreciated the compliment all the same. She placed her pile of clothing on the counter and Zilzina tossed the leather pants on top. "Um, it's not too much, is it?" the cambion asked. She'd only been in small general stores with her mother before and didn't have a great grasp of money, just that Zilzina was short of it at the moment.

"Not a problem," Diona replied and slipped a few coins to the attendant who was bundling everything with a length of twine. "Did you add in the mask?"

"No miss, not from here. I thought it yours," said the dwarf, looking at Autumn.

"No, your aide gave it to me," replied the girl. "The elven man."

The dwarf frowned. "Aide? I have no aide."

Zilzina and Autumn shared a glance. "Who gave that to you?" the hunter asked. She scanned the showroom but no one else was there.

"I didn't get his name."

***

Diona led them through the still bustling city to her home, which she explained was an orphanage. She took in unfortunate children from Laguton and the surrounding villages. It wasn't dissimilar from what Serah had done for Zilzina, though as they approached the hunter noted that Diona was much better funded. The house was a mansion on the west side of town, complete with sprawling, if overgrown, grounds and a wrought iron gate.

According to Diona, the building housed twenty-four souls, mostly children, though she did have a small staff. As they walked in through the large double doors, Autumn was awestruck. She'd never seen a place like this, with expensive looking furniture, fine art, and fragile vases lining the entry hall. Thinking back to her own childhood, not all that long ago, the girl wondered how often the vases had to be replaced in a house with more than a dozen children.

Light bulbs buzzed in fixtures along the wall and a fire roared in the large hearth of what must be the common room. It seemed like the best place in the world to Autumn, who had never known anything other than rough cabins, seedy inns, and the open road with Zilzina. A number of children milled about the room, playing with toys, reading books, and idling by the fire.

"Didi!" a small girl squealed and ran down the staircase across from them. She leapt into Diona's open arms.

"Hey cupcake," Diona said, picking the girl up and pinching her cheek. "You miss me?"

The girl nodded, chanting. "Bath, bath, bath."

Diona laughed. "You are the only one in this house that likes the bath."

"Madame, welcome back," an elderly elf woman said as she descended the stairs. She wore a black and white uniform. "I see you have found her for me."

"Hello Yona, yes." Diona gestured toward Zilzina and Autumn. "These are our guests for the night. Would you see about finding rooms for them? I will get the baths started."

A groan rose up from the children milling about the room, several of the younger ones even running to hide behind furniture. The older children sighed and began rounding them up in a practiced ritual. It seemed bath time was quite the operation in this household. Zilzina felt woefully out of place, drawing her cloak tighter to hide the weapons hanging from her belt. Autumn, on the other hand, was rather enjoying herself.

As he was being herded upstairs, a boy stopped and pointed at Autumn's mask. "Scary," he said matter-of-factly.

"Janten, that's not polite," said Diona. "Say you're sorry."

"Sorry." He didn't look particularly apologetic.

Autumn paused for a moment then, with a grin hidden by the mask, and gave a mock roar that sent the child running up the stairs. She was still laughing when Diona passed her, chuckling to herself, and Zilzina smacked her on the back of the head.

"Now that wasn't polite," the elf said. "Maybe you need to stay here for a bit and learn some manners."

Diona had paused at the bottom of the stairs and was looking over at an orc girl, probably not much younger than

Autumn, who still sat, sulking, in a plush chair in the corner. "No luck today, sweetie?"

The orc shook her head and pulled farther back into the cushions.

"Tomorrow will be better," the caretaker continued. "Come on now, go have a bath."

Once the girl had slipped shyly up the stairs, Zilzina asked, "who is she?"

"She was the only survivor of a demon attack on a small settlement not far from Laguton. We still don't know her name. She hasn't said a word since she arrived."

How awful, Autumn thought. "She seems so distant."

"Well," Diona replied. "That's part of why you are here."

"What do you mean?" asked Zilzina, her senses prickling.

"For several nights now, we've had… incidents."

"Incidents?" Zilzina repeated. "What does that mean?"

"Well, several children have gone missing," Diona sighed. "Now runaways aren't that uncommon, even from here, and the authorities don't have the time to deal with every urchin who goes missing. But this isn't the same. We've heard strange sounds in the hallways at night."

"I see. Do you have any evidence that it's a demon?"

"Nothing, other than the disappearance's starting when the girl arrived. The other children have got it into their heads that she's the demon or working with it. I know better, of course. She's just a sweet girl who needs some time to heal. But it is worrisome all the same."

Autumn couldn't blame the children but made sure her mask was tightly fastened.

"They may not be far off," Zilzina said. "Whether or not it's the girl there's a good chance the demon is already in the house, otherwise there would be some sign of entry. Autumn, do you smell anything?"

The cambion sniffed for a moment and shook her head. None of that sickening undercurrent of rot that lingered in the air wherever a demon went. In fact, there wasn't much scent at all, save for her and Zilzina. Even Diona's human smell was faded.

Diona also smelled the air, though her senses were of no use in a situation like this. "In the house?" she exclaimed. "How could that be?"

"A shapeshifter, perhaps," replied the hunter. "They're rare but do exist."

"I've never heard of that."

Autumn hadn't either.

"They can take the form of others," Zilzina continued. "I've tracked one before. They're tough to pin down and tend to hide in unexpected places, such as an orphanage. It may even have followed the orc girl here."

"It could be anywhere?" Diona was verging on panic.

"Calm down, that won't help anything." Zilzina checked her pistol. "Just tell me about the disappearances."

"There have been two," replied the matron with a deep breath. "All in the last week, since the girl arrived. We still don't know her name... Hartley and Jambion, both taken in the dead of night. The children say they heard, well, a demon in the hall. Growls and creaking, that sort of thing."

Autumn could feel that sickening knot begin to form in her stomach, a feeling that was becoming all too familiar.

"Don't worry," Zilzina said calmly. "We'll find it. I promise."

***

Yona showed Zilzina and Autumn to a moderately sized room and brought in a late dinner. It was far better accommodations than either had experienced in some time—for Autumn, probably ever. There was even a bath which Yona had already warmed. Despite the potential danger at hand, even Zilzina couldn't say no to that and took a dip once Autumn had finished. The grime of the road washed away with a pleasant-smelling soap.

Once the elf was finished, she returned to the main room to find Autumn sprawled out on the plush, sizable bed. She lay on her back and flipped through a large tome from the tall bookcase in the corner. After the bath, she noticed that she could sense everyone normally again. Maybe she'd just smelled that bad from the road before.

Zilzina posted up in a chair near the door, intent on remaining alert through the night in case of another occurrence. She spent several minutes conducting a now ritualistic inspection of her weapons and settled in.

"Hey Zilzina?" Autumn called after some time had passed. "How did demons come about?"

"Hmm…" she mused while polishing her tri-barreled pistol. "Demons are… chaotic beings. According to legend, the gods once protected the world from the influence of Chaos. That was before some idiot killed them anyway."

"That's vague, how could a mortal slay a god?" Autumn asked, putting her book down.

"I'm not sure," replied Zilzina. "There are a number of myths for how the demons first came. Some say the oni called them here and were given a drop of the Chaos as reward, changing them."

"That makes sense."

"As do many myths, but no one can say for certain which is true, and which is not."

"What is the difference between a devil and a demon then?" Autumn could feel her eyelids getting heavy but was determined to make the most of the talkative mood Zilzina seemed to be in. The hunter rarely answered her questions on this subject.

"Devils are weaker than demons, and lesser devils even more so, though they can evolve to become more powerful by consuming mortals." There was a scrape at the window, causing Zilzina to tense but it was just a waving branch.

"I see. Are there many other forms?"

"Demons, higher demons, and, of course, cambions," Zilzina replied, looking Autumn's way. "The higher demons are forces of nature. They've spent centuries consuming and evolving, becoming unimaginably powerful."

"Was…" Autumn found it hard to say. "… was my father a higher demon?"

Zilzina scoffed. "Hardly."

"He seemed powerful when you fought."

"No, I was just weak. I hadn't fed for a long time." Her stomach growled at the reminder, the last chance to feed having been when they stayed with Martha and Klaus. The closer they moved to the city, the harder it would be to find demons. Frankly, Diona's plight was a potential godsend to the cursed elf.

"You always say that," Autumn said sleepily. She stifled a yawn.

"Get some sleep."

The cambion intended to protest but was already nodding off. The next thing she knew was when she was being shaken gently awake. The fire in their room had died down and it was pitch black outside.

"Get up and be quiet," Zilzina whispered. "Something is happening out there."

Just then, a child's scream split the silence. Autumn fumbled with her mask as Zilzina bolted out of the room, pistol in hand. Down the hall from them, the door to the children's room stood open, pale moonlight pouring through it and illuminating the orc girl. She was dragging the human boy, Janten, out by his collar as he thrashed and screamed.

Zilzina and Autumn ran forward, drawing new cries of terror from Janten–he'd already made his thoughts on Autumn's mask clear and Zilzina was a frightful sight under the circumstances. He was bleeding from three gashes on his left leg. The orc girl let go of him and cowered in the corner as Diona appeared from down the hall.

"Come on, it's ok," Autumn said, beckoning to the boy.

He looked at her and winced, then stood and hobbled over to Zilzina, who knelt down to inspect his leg. His cries grew louder as the shock passed from his system.

"What is going on?" Diona shouted. She carried a small lamp, bathing the scene in a flickering orange glow.

"The wounds are deep, but he will heal," Zilzina said, ignoring the child's clinging. "Autumn, see that they are wrapped."

Autumn stepped forward and picked up the crying child.

"Shh, it's okay," she said. "I won't hurt you." He seemed to calm a bit as she took him back to their room to find a cloth.

"I- I- I told you she was a demon," he managed between hiccups and pointed.

The orc girl was still cowering in the corner, shaking her head.

"No," Zilzina said as she stood. "I don't think she is. Diona, will you sit with the children? Keep them in their room-"

Another scream sounded from the first floor. Before Zilzina could spring into action, Yona came rushing up the stairs, her hands and dress covered in blood.

"Madame Diona," the aging elf said in a dry voice. "The cook…"

***

It was a while before a semblance of calm settled again over the house. Zilzina and Diona were able to convince the children that the orc girl had actually saved Janten, pulling him away when someone or something had tried to take him. Diona tried signaling the police but her telegraph–an incredible invention that Zilzina might have marveled at in other circumstances–had been smashed.

"We need to send for help," the matron said for perhaps the fourth time.

"It's too dangerous until morning," replied Zilzina again.

95

She understood the woman's concern, but her patience was growing thin. She did not normally work directly with the clients for a reason. "The demon could be out there, waiting to pick off whoever goes. And if I leave it may simply attack the rest of you. Not to mention herding everyone to leave at once would be just as dangerous. I can protect you better here. We have to be patient."

They all sat huddled in the main room with a large fire going. Zilzina had investigated the pantry where the cook lay, dead, obviously the victim of a feeding frenzy. She'd gone through the rooms of the first floor, barring doors and windows, and dragged several pieces of furniture into blocking positions. It wasn't ideal but this would have to do.

"I'm sorry," she said to Diona as the woman tried to hush one of the crying children. "I should have been there earlier."

A tear was rolling down the matron's cheek from her red veined eyes. "Just find it and end this. Please."

Zilzina nodded solemnly.

"It killed someone this time. What changed?" Autumn whispered so the children wouldn't hear.

"Someone interrupted its meal," replied Zilzina.

Yona appeared just then from the kitchen with a tray of tea. She'd taken some time to clean up, scrubbing the blood from her hands and changing clothes, and insisted that she would be safe enough in the room next door to prepare tea.

"Thank you," Zilzina murmured, accepting a cup and sipping mildly.

"You're welcome," the elderly elf replied. She turned to Autumn and offered her a cup as well.

"Thank... you," breathed the girl. Yona's hands were clean. Immaculate. She must have used soap and scrubbed hard. But she didn't smell like an elf. She didn't smell like anything. As the caretaker moved through the room, distributing cups, Autumn moved closer to Zilzina and lowered her voice. "Can you smell Yona?"

"What... no, I can't." Zilzina's eye's narrowed as she turned slightly to watch Yona.

"It's strange, even now everyone else's scent is fading too, almost like-"

"Like a mask. Autumn, get everyone out of here." Zilzina stood and drew her silver dagger. "Hey Yona, take this. In case, the demon shows up," she continued, tossing the weapon to Yona.

The elderly elf caught the dagger reflexively but dropped it right away. Her hand was instantly singed and smoking.

"Autumn, get them out of here, now!" the hunter shouted.

"Clever," Yona said, her voice deepening and contorting as her body did the same. She grew at least a foot, and her skin took on a cracked, charcoal hue. Her eyes, which were now slitted like a lizard, were bright yellow. "Now what, elf?"

Diona screamed in horror as Autumn gathered her and the children and raced toward the back door. With a flourish, Zilzina brought her pistol up to fire, but the demon was too quick. Even before she could pull the trigger, Zilzina felt the blow that knocked her weapon aside. It clattered down the hall, misfiring all but the last three rounds of silvered ammunition Zilzina had left in her belt. This was going to be a tough one.

Seeing the hunter on the backfoot, Autumn rushed forward from the hall where Diona and the children were escaping. She grabbed Zilzina's dagger from the floor–luckily simple contact with silver didn't seem to affect her–and tossed it to the embattled elf. "Catch," she said, taking cover behind the couch.

Zilzina saw the flash of silver and managed to duck under the demon's next blow. She reached for the spinning weapon but was knocked aside when Yona, or whatever it was, followed through with a powerful leg sweep. The dagger went clattering down the hallway after the pistol.

"A pitiful display," the demon said, grappling Zilzina and pinning her down. "From the way you and the girl carried yourselves, I expected more of a fight."

Autumn edged her way carefully around the couch and into the hall. The demon was focused on Zilzina, who was still struggling somewhat effectively. She had to get that dagger.

"I hadn't wanted to reveal myself so soon," the demon hissed. It pinned Zilzina's leg, but the hunter managed to wriggle an arm free. "No one misses a few orphans here and there. This house was like a larder!"

"You're despicable," Zilzina shouted. She saw Autumn creep down the hall and pick up her dagger again. Their eyes met and the elf signaled to wait with her free hand. "Even for your kind, that's low."

"My kind?" hissed the fiend. Its forked tongue flicked, tasting the air. "You're one to talk! Tell me, when was the last time you fed? You know the pleasure."

With a surge of adrenaline, Zilzina pushed herself up and into the demon, knocking it off balance. She managed to drive it into the wall near the fireplace and held her hand up. "Autumn, now!"

Autumn said a quick blessing and threw the dagger as hard as she could. It glinted in the earlier morning light, spinning through beams of sunlight appearing with the then rising sun as Zilzina wrestled with the beast in the corner. It seemed an eternity, the weapon hanging there in the still air, their lives hanging in the balance. Then all at once it was over. Zilzina snatched the silver dagger out of the air and slammed it into the demon's chest with both hands. She put her whole body into driving the point in through the scaly, charcoal hide.

And, with a roar and a spray of hot blood, what had once been Yona died.

Zilzina breathed heavily, still hunched over the demon's corpse. She looked up when Autumn approached, veins standing out in her neck and the violet glow bright in her eyes. She was doing everything she could to hold back from feeding. "Go," the hunter said with ragged breaths. "Keep them out."

Autumn nodded and rushed outside. She burst through the door and told Diona that everything was okay. Zilzina would take care of the fiend.

She didn't want to imagine what the feeding was like, but Zilzina's twisted features as she sat over the demon's corpse was burned into her mind. Autumn slid down against the wall and waited.

***

The next morning, a repairman was busy at work righting the damage Zilzina had done to the first floor. As she and Autumn descended the staircase, Diona glided over to them joyfully, though a somber glaze held in her eyes.

"Thank you, both of you, so much," she said, handing them each a fresh fig and cheese hand pie. "I just can't... thank you enough."

"Don't mention it," Zilzina said. She cleared her throat expectantly.

"Ah, yes, the rest of your payment," continued Diona. She pulled a pouch out of her pocket and offered it to the elf. "Just one question, was Yona always…?"

"No," replied Zilzina, taking the pouch. "Shapeshifters can only shift into those they've killed, unfortunately."

"Oh, I see…"

"Didi!" The small girl from before came rushing down the stairs, straight to Diona. Once she'd been lifted into her caretaker's arms, she turned and saw Zilzina counting down the pouch. "Coins," the girl said matter-of-factly.

"We couldn't possibly accept-" Autumn began, her mouth full of delicious fig and cheese. She lifted her mask slightly to take another bite.

"- any more than this, thank you," Zilzina finished for her. She stuffed the pouch in her pack and ruffled the cambion's hair.

Autumn frowned but busied herself with finishing the hand pie.

"Of course, don't be strangers," Diona said, following them to the door. "You're sure you won't stay longer? You are most welcome here any time."

Ignoring Autumn's pleading eyes, Zilzina shook her head. "No, I'm afraid we must be off to Sapoul. If you're ever in trouble though, you can use that fancy machine of yours to wire Serah in the warehouse district there. She'll know how to contact me."

"Serah in the warehouse district," Diona repeated. "Farewell, Autumn and Zilzina. I do hope we meet again."

"Bye!" Autumn called, waving back to the children that were gathering out front to see them off.

As was her style, Zilzina did not turn back. She did, however, offer a halfhearted backward wave in response to the chorus of goodbyes. *Shit*, Autumn was making her soft.

CHAPTER V

"Stay close," Zilzina warned, sensing Autumn drifting away from her. "Keep to the sidewalk."

"I'm not going to run away," sighed the girl without looking. The closer they got to Sapoul the more interesting the locales grew, and Crimson Town was no exception. There was a diverse mix of people crowding the sidewalks, pressing and jostling into Autumn. She'd never really been in a crowd before, especially not one that never seemed to end.

"I know you won't run away. I'm just telling you to be careful," Zilzina continued. She could feel Autumn rolling her eyes beneath the mask. It wasn't that she liked being so stern but the more they traveled through the populous areas, the more dangerous it was for Autumn, and the girl possessed a sort of idle recklessness that Zilzina couldn't wrap her head around. Sure, she was young, but Autumn's curiosity seemed to rule her actions altogether.

"I'm tired," the cambion complained after a while.

"When are you not?"

"You know, a little 'good work walking for two days without any proper rest, Autumn' would go a long way. Might give me a second wind."

"Good work walking for two days without any rest." Zilzina paused and held her arm out to stop Autumn at the street corner. A motor vehicle passed and they continued.

"I'm still tired. We should get one of those," the girl continued.

"What, a motor carriage?" Zilzina laughed. "Do you know how much work those machines are? They're hardly any good anywhere outside of the city. Not to mention how expensive they are."

A "hmph" was all Autumn warranted for a reply, more out of stubbornness than a genuine disappointment. Of course they couldn't get a vehicle like that. She trailed along in a zigzag pattern as Zilzina led the way to an inn down the street. The hunter had obviously been here before.

The doorbell jingled loudly as they pushed inside. The bottom floor was a dim taproom filled largely with middle-aged men of various races sitting at long tables. Each of them glanced at the newcomers but the general murmur of conversation skipped only a beat before the patrons returned to their business. Zilzina pulled her hood tighter, her violet eyes glimmering beneath, and Autumn did the same.

"This is kinda-" the girl began but Zilzina cut her off.

"Don't say anything unnecessary."

A stern looking elven man stood behind the counter, cleaning mugs. He eyed them suspiciously and grunted, "what can I get you?" as they approached.

"A room for two," Zilzina replied.

He stared at them for a few moments before continuing. "What is it with you two?"

"That's a bit rude," Autumn couldn't help herself from replying. She bowed her head shamefully at Zilzina's quick glare.

"I can't just let anyone in here. I'm sure you understand, it's my job to ask a few questions," the innkeeper said. "Safety and all that, right?

Zilzina did not understand but she kept that to herself. "If you're worried we'll be any trouble, I assure you we won't. My sister and I are just looking for a place to stay the night."

"Anyone could say that you know," replied the elven man. "In fact, they all do."

Having made up her mind that this was a waste of time, Zilzina turned to leave just as another voice cut in.

"You're being too harsh, father," a younger elf chided. He stepped out from the back room, wiping his hands with a cloth and then stuffing it into his apron. "Bad for business to treat a customer that way."

"Son, I've been doing this a long time. What's bad for business is taking in such strangers with no explanation." The man emphasized the strange part of the word strangers.

The younger elf waved off his father's words and pulled his dark hair out of the messy ponytail he'd had it up in. "It's the style to be strange these days, father. You'd know that if you ever got out." His red eyes flicked from Autumn's mask to Zilzina's face, their gazes locking for a moment. "And besides, they're quite lovely."

"Stop flirting," an older elven woman said with mild annoyance as she stepped out of the same room–probably the kitchen–that the young man had. She reached up to smack the back of his head, but he dodged away playfully. "I'm sorry sweety, we try to teach him manners but it's no use."

"Ouch, gentle mother!"

"Don't worry about it," Zilzina said, her voice droll. She wasn't interested in the compliments, only getting a room.

Nearby patrons chuckled at the scene. The mother mock sparred with her son for a minute or so, to the crowd's continued amusement and her husband's obvious annoyance, before patting him on the arm and returning to her station. Despite his frown, the innkeeper's mood had lightened somewhat, and he pulled a heavy key from a hook behind him.

"I suppose there's no harm in it," he said, walking toward the stairs. "Come along.

Zilzina started toward the stairs but turned back when Autumn didn't follow. The cambion was looking toward the innkeeper's son, who in turn seemed enamored with Zilzina. "Come on," the hunter said and grabbed Autumn's hand. They followed the innkeeper upstairs, feeling his son's eyes on them the whole way.

"We've only got the expensive room left," the older elf said as he led them through the second-floor hallway. He unlocked one of the doors and showed them inside. "Big, good lighting, private bath. Can you afford it?"

"Yes," replied Zilzina, slipping a few coins out from her pouch, still heavy with Diona's bounty. Once the innkeeper was gone, Zilzina put a finger to lips, motioning for Autumn to stay quiet. She removed her coat and jacket, drawing up her sleeve to reveal the intricate tattoos underneath.

The hunter used her fang-like teeth to puncture her thumb and smeared a drop of blood on one of the symbols. A numb tingle radiated from her arm, and she continued the spell by putting drops of blood on the door and each window. Once the spell was complete, she nodded to Autumn, who had already taken off her mask.

"That was magic, wasn't it?" the girl said. She stepped

forward and looked closely at Zilzina's arm.

"Yes. No one can hear us from outside the room now."

"Cool. We should use magic more often." Autumn hopped up on the bed and started working her boots off.

"I only have a few spells, that one Serah taught me. And like I said, it's dark magic. It uses my own life force and should be reserved for special situations."

"Right," continued Autumn. She was rustling through their pack now. "Are you worried someone out there will spy on us?"

"You never know." Zilzina walked around the room again, inspecting the cabinets and drawers. "The owner wasn't particularly friendly, and his son was obnoxious."

"Yeah... he seemed sort of familiar somehow."

"Odd. Anyway," continued the hunter, pulling a stoppered bottle out of one of the cabinets and smelling it deeply. "The expensive room has its perks."

"Is that shampoo?" Autumn rushed over excitedly.

"Come on, I'll wash your hair."

***

After washing, the pair lounged in the main room, Zilzina in a chair by the window and Autumn on the bed reading a book that had somehow fallen into their bag from Diona's house. Not that Zilzina generally minded a bit of petty theft, but the woman had been kind to them. She'd made Autumn promise to return it via post once they reached Serah's.

"Hey, uh, Zilzina?" Autumn said after a bit of fidgeting.

"Hmm?"

"I've been wondering about something..." The girl hesitated.

"Yes?"

"Well, uh, I've read some books about, you know, adult stuff..."

Here we go, Zilzina thought.

"You know, like what a man does with his-"

"Yes, I know," Zilzina interjected. This was more uncomfortable than facing down a vicious foe. "What about it?"

"Why did my mother do something like that with a demon?"

Zilzina stared out the window for a few minutes without answering. She wasn't even sure how to answer. There were a number of possibilities, the most probable of which were not pleasant. "I think," she said at last. "I think only your mother would know that."

"I did ask her once," replied Autumn somberly. "But she only got sad and didn't answer. I know I should just leave it alone but..."

"You're curious," Zilzina finished. "I understand, I feel the same way about my own curse. Not that you're cursed, I mean-"

"It's okay, I know what you meant."

"And what's really important is everything else she did for you."

"I know," Autumn sighed. "I just wish she was still here."

"Yeah, me too."

They sat in silence again for some time after that, Zilzina sharpening her dagger and Autumn flipping through her book. Eventually, a soft knock sounded at the door. With a groan, Zilzina got up and walked over.

"Ah, hello," the innkeeper's son said from the other side.

"What do you want?" Zilzina replied in her well-practiced monotone.

"I thought you might like something to eat," he continued.

Zilzina glanced over at Autumn who was already fastening her mask and putting her coat on. Once the cambion was ready, Zilzina fixed her hair and opened the door part way. The young, red-eyed elf stood there, a bit taller than Zilzina. He was... rather handsome if she were to be honest with herself, though he gave her a strange feeling. And she didn't often go in for that sort of thing.

"Hi," he said, smiling.

"You said something about food?"

"Straight to the point, I like that." His laugh was almost becoming.

Zilzina shook her head to clear it. "So…?"

"Take a walk with me." He offered her his hand.

"Right. No, that's okay," said the hunter shortly. "I have to keep an eye on my sister. We're tired from the road, need to call it an early night." Zilzina was getting annoyed, but at the same time…

"We could stay another night," Autumn piped up, much to her caretaker's chagrin. She was more than happy to extend their time off the road before they reached Serah's and Zilzina would go her own way.

"Perfect, tomorrow evening then!" the young elf piped up.

Autumn felt Zilzina staring daggers at her, but she took no heed. This whole encounter was quite entertaining to her. "I'll make sure she's ready."

"Fine," Zilzina muttered. "And about food tonight?"

The young elf laughed. "I'll bring something up. Is there anything else you require?"

"Books!" Autumn said quickly.

"Books it is." He bowed and sidled away.

"What's your name?" Zilzina called as he started walking down the stairs.

The younger elf paused and turned back with a grin. "That is a secret."

Rolling her eyes, Zilzina shut the door and returned to her chair. She ignored Autumn's giggles. That girl was going to be the death of her.

"So," the cambion began. "Am I to believe he was, how do they say it, wooing you?"

"Shut up. I probably won't even go. This whole situation is ridiculous."

Autumn just smiled and returned to her book. It wasn't until then that Zilzina noted that the innkeeper's son had heard and talked to her from beyond the sound barrier. With a sigh, she stood up to recast the spell–she must have made a mistake the first time.

**

Autumn spent all night reading one of the three books the innkeeper's son had brought. Then she slept for half the next day, only to wake up and start reading again.

It was no wonder she was well learned despite living apart from society. She tried to get Zilzina to read one of the other books, but the hunter turned her down. Books were not her thing.

"Preparing for your red-eyed prince's arrival?" Autumn mocked as Zilzina exercised in the corner.

"You're really annoying, you know that?" she huffed between crunches. "There's something off about him. I probably won't even go."

The electric lamplights were flickering outside when a knock sounded at the door. The hunter got up and fixed her silver hair, caught up in a tight braid Autumn had shown her how to do. "Just don't say anything, okay?" she continued, sighing when Autumn simply wiggled her eyebrows and slipped her mask on.

"Good evening," the innkeeper's son said when Zilzina opened the door. He was dressed in a red buttoned shirt and dark trousers. A jacket was draped over his arm. He looked innocent enough, perhaps a short walk wouldn't be so bad, Zilzina thought. At least she could have a bit of company that wasn't a stubborn, adolescent cambion for a while.

"Hi," the hunter replied. She was flushed and out of breath from exercise.

"That happy to see me?" the younger elf winked.

Zilzina rolled her eyes and looked back to Autumn. "I'll ask them to bring up some food. And-"

"I know, I know, stay here. I will. Go have fun."

"Uh huh," Zilzina replied, unsure of anything Autumn had just said. "Lock this after us." She pulled her hood up and led the way, closing the door behind her. "Are we walking anywhere in particular?"

"It's a walk," the younger elf replied. "We don't need a destination."

"Why would you want to do something so aimless?"

He gestured toward her. "Because I am allowed to do so with you."

Zilzina didn't reply but rather fell into step with the innkeeper's son, a frustratingly slow meander compared to her normal pace. She was used to hunting, to moving with purpose. Rather than dwell on the annoyance, however, she took in the sights. Crimson was nothing special but there was some interesting architecture. She had been here before but had not spent much time just... walking.

"Why are you so bothered about whether or not you are seen?" asked the younger elf after some time. Zilzina still had her hood up and moved in a generally furtive manner.

"You might be too if you looked like this," she responded, gesturing to her face. Her pale, nearly white, skin framed slightly glowing violet eyes. "Are you not bothered by it?"

"No, do you want me to be bothered?"

"What? No, I don't care. That's up to you,"

"True," he laughed. "It doesn't mean I don't notice things you try to hide. The fangs for one, though you do a good job of keeping that one hidden. And the skin and eyes are obvious. I think you're quite beautiful."

"Right." Zilzina felt oddly flushed. What was she doing? This was the sort of clumsy pickup line she'd heard a dozen times before. There were always those in taverns that were into freaks, that thought they made easy prey. Still, somehow this felt different–for some reason it was working. "You're a strange one."

"Am I now? Perhaps we're all strange," he replied, guiding her down another well-lit street. "Frigia has two main hubs, the twin cities of Sapoul and Miesot. From afar, one might praise how far they have developed in culture and technology and how that development has spread to the surrounding area. From my perspective, however, they are testaments to the decline that technology brings. Frigia neglects the people for progress, allowing them to dig a hole of ancient grudges that will bury the empire in the end."

"Is this the sort of thing people generally speak of on walks?" Zilzina joked. What was she doing? She actually felt herself smile a bit.

"No, not typically, but then you aren't a typical woman."

"Well, I'm not much interested in the well-being of the empire," said Zilzina. "It's all squabbling politicians clawing their way to the top. They ignore the needs of their people. Hunger, sickness, and demons are rampant across Frigia, and the empire isn't doing a damned thing."

"Perhaps someone ought to do something about them. The politicians, that is. You seem to have the demon's handled."

"How do you know…" she started. They turned to face each other, Zilzina's stare inquisitive as she studied his sharp features.

"It was just a guess," he replied. "Though now I know for sure."

Zilzina sighed and started walking again, ahead of the innkeeper's son.

"I see many kinds of people," he continued, jogging to catch up. "And few are armed as you are, save mercenaries and hunters. And given your interest in the well-being of people I didn't take you for a mercenary. Not to mention the girl, your sister."

"Well, I prefer not to advertise that, if you don't mind."

"My lips are sealed," he said and pointed to a small shop a block from them. "How about a pastry? I did promise you food, after all."

The shop had an open-air counter facing the sidewalk. Behind it was a vast number of breads and pastries on racks, and behind those, ovens and equipment being put to use to make more. A line of customers extended nearly down the block, but it moved quickly. Once they arrived at the window, the innkeeper's son asked for "jam bread" and Zilzina ordered the same. When she moved to pay, he just laughed and gently pushed her arm away, pulling his own pouch out.

"The gentleman is expected to pay on a walk," he explained.

Zilzina simply rolled her eyes and took a bite of the jam bread. It was delicious. They walked for a while longer, eating their fill of the pastry, before she broke the silence. "I really can't just keep calling you innkeeper's son."

"You never did."

"Well, that's what I call you when I think."

"You think about me?" he turned and beamed. "You can call me whatever you like."

"Why not your real name?"

"I told you, it's a secret."

"This is getting childish," she muttered but continued walking. "I'll just call you whatever."

"I like being childish, it's fun," he replied. "So, no ideas on what to call me then?"

"Whatever," Zilzina said again.

"Wait, you can't actually call me whatever."

"Can I call you your real name?"

"Well, no…"

Zilzina shrugged. "Then I'll call you Whatever."

"You're impossible," he replied, dejected.

Zilzina laughed a bit at his annoyance. "Don't worry, I know someone much more childish."

"Oh, you've got some jam on your face," he said, reaching toward her face

She stepped back and attempted to lick it off, her tongue moving like a chameleon's. She knew it must look ridiculous.

"Not quite, here, let me." He stepped close and leaned in, stopping short, expectantly.

Zilzina reached up and wiped the jam away. "In your

dreams," she said and licked it from her thumb as she continued their journey. "We should get more of that jam bread."

The innkeeper's son simply shook his head and followed. "Okay, but this time, you're paying."

***

Autumn glanced sidelong at the pots stacked on the bedside table. "I'm hungry," she said, setting her book down and sitting up. Dinner for her and Zilzina had already been delivered–she hadn't bothered telling them it was only her–but her stomach still rumbled. She was a growing girl after all.

Where was Zilzina anyway? She'd been out a long time. Hopefully that was a good thing. The girl just realized that she hadn't really been alone since Zilzina had found her. She missed the elf's quiet brooding and the way she got annoyed at Autumn. But everyone deserved some time to themselves. All of Zilzina's time had been spent on Autumn these past few weeks. Yes, she hoped the hunter was having fun.

None of that helped Autumn's hunger though. Her stomach rumbled again. She was tempted to head downstairs and ask for another plate. Tonight, they were serving potted pies and they were delicious.

Zilzina would understand. She was really hungry.

Autumn hopped off the bed and slipped her coat over her undergarments–she didn't feel like getting properly dressed.

Grabbing her mask and fastening it she walked to the door, opening it slowly. She slipped her gloves on and took a step out. It was exhilarating–she'd never been out in public on her own.

"What are you doing?"

Autumn whipped around. Before her was a young elf, a girl who looked about her age but was likely much older. The various races of Frigia aged very differently. Klaus had been in his late twenties when he… But this wasn't the time for that. Autumn composed herself and replied. "Umm, nothing."

"It looked like you were creeping out of your room," the elf girl continued, cocking her head.

Now that Autumn considered it, why did she have to sneak? No one else would care that she was out of the room. "Well… I'm not."

"Okay. I'm Gaia."

"Hi, I'm Autumn." This was weird, but Autumn resolved to act as normal as possible, whatever that meant.

"Why are you wearing a mask?"

"I was going to get food from downstairs."

"Oh!" The girl jumped in excitement. "My mom is in the kitchen, I'll take you."

"Okay, let's go!" Autumn figured it would be better to be accompanied by the girl so no one asked her questions. Plus, she didn't actually have any money. How lucky, of all the people to meet it was the daughter of the inn's owners. As the pair headed down to the kitchen, Autumn hoped that Zilzina did not get back before she'd gotten her food. The hunter would lock her up next time if she found out.

***

It was late by the time Zilzina returned. There were a handful of patrons still scattered about the tavern, but no one took much notice of their entry.

"Father," the young elf, Whatever, greeted the innkeeper.

"Finally back," he replied, eyeing the hooded Zilzina and nodding.

Zilzina returned the nod. The older elf was obviously still suspicious but was at least keeping it to himself now. Not to mention she and Autumn would be gone in the morning.

"Where's Gaia?" Whatever asked.

"Maybe in the kitchen. She was around earlier."

"I'll be down soon," continued the innkeeper's son, casually putting a hand on Zilzina's back and leading her toward the stairs.

The hunter quickened her pace, stepping away from the hand, and made her way upstairs unassisted. Regardless of the intention, Whatever's actions were still annoying. "Who's Gaia?" she asked to break the slightly awkward silence that followed.

"My younger sister." Whatever sounded a bit sullen but

not dejected.

When they reached Zilzina's room she lowered her hood and looked at the innkeeper's son mildly. He was waiting expectantly.

"Did you... enjoy yourself?" he said after a moment.

"It was... okay. I would have preferred staying indoors," she said, noting the look of disappointment in the younger elf's face. "Though I didn't hate it."

"I suppose that's high praise, coming from you," he chuckled.

"I suppose it is." She paused, her hand on the door handle. "Well... I guess I'll see you later."

Whatever nodded but remained standing there expectantly.

Zilzina started to turn the handle, then stopped and sighed. "What?"

"What what?"

"Well, you're just staring. What do you want?"

He smiled and walked to the door opposite Zilzina's room, slipping a key out of his pocket and unlocking it. "Can I show you something?"

An invitation. Zilzina looked hesitant at her own door then to Whatever, who stood in the now open doorway to the opposite room. His red eyes sparkled in the warm lamplight. "Okay," she said at last and stepped past him inside the other room. *What the hell am I doing?* It was modest compared to hers. And there was, without a doubt, nothing here to see.

"Well," she continued. "What did you want to show me?"

"What do you want to see?" he quipped, following her inside and shutting the door.

Zilzina dragged her palms over her face and laughed. "This is ridiculous."

The innkeeper's son stepped forward, a little too close, though there wasn't much room for Zilzina to back up. "But it's fun, isn't it?" he asked, touching her forearm.

The hunter shivered involuntarily, drawing a fresh grin from her ever-smiling host. She shivered again when he leaned close to speak near her pointed ear.

"Do you dislike how you feel, ridiculous though my methods may be?" He ventured a soft kiss on her neck. "Do you not enjoy the… warmth?"

Zilzina jumped back when she felt the younger elf starting to slip her coat off. She could indeed feel the warmth in her core, a stark contrast to her naturally frigid body temperature. She also vividly recalled the last time someone besides Autumn had seen her tattoos.

"Okay," she said, centering herself. "I'm not doing this."

The innkeeper's son sat on the bed and watched as she walked past him to stand by the door. "What bothers you?" he asked.

"I don't even know your name."

"That's not what bothers you. You're the kind of person who would rather move through life as a shadow, not knowing or being known by anyone."

He read her too well and that made her uncomfortable. "I don't have to explain myself to you. I'm not doing this." She reached for the door.

"Really, has it been that long?"

She paused, looking at the floor and chuckling humorlessly. Am I doing this? She thought, turning to the still expectant younger elf, Whatever.

"Okay," she said at last.

Throwing her coat aside and slipping out of her shirt, she stood in front of him. He looked her up and down, an appraisal.

"Adorable tattoos," he remarked, slipping his own shirt off. The innkeeper's son was similarly tattooed, black magic and all, though his ink covered the majority of his torso. "Though you have a bit of catching up to do."

Zilzina raised her brows. This was... interesting. "Where did you get those?"

"Come now, I may be in this little shithole now, but I've seen the world," he said. "I've done things."

Interesting indeed. This was different than she'd imagined.

"I can smell your desire."

Any race gifted with an exceptional sense of smell could do that, especially with fear and sex hormones. Right now, Zilzina could smell the change within him as well.

"I don't know what the big deal is." He drummed his fingers on the side table. "I just want a good fuck."

That did it. This meant nothing. It was just that, a good fuck. A casual night with someone who she would never meet again. She didn't like to admit it, but she needed this. She walked over and straddled the younger elf. He let out a deep growl.

They locked eyes for a moment, violet on red. Then he kissed her, his emotion more feral than she'd anticipated. Flipping her onto the bed he paused. "I'm far from gentle," he warned.

"Try me."

***

"I need a bath," Zilzina announced as she and Whatever-his-name-was lay in bed an hour later, staring at the ceiling.

"Perhaps I should join you?" he purred, biting her shoulder.

Tempting as it was… "I'll be fine on my own, thanks."

He laughed. "Okay then."

The hunter sat up, looking for her clothes. As she gathered them up, she caught sight of a slip of paper on the side table. "Is this a bounty?" she asked, picking it up to examine. It described a four-armed demon harassing the surrounding area. The reward was not insubstantial. That money would go a long way for Serah.

"It is," the elf said, sounding bored. "It's been attacking travelers and the outskirts of Crimson. You're not actually thinking about going after it?"

"That's my business," she said and started getting dressed.

"Come on now, two hunters have already been killed going after it," he continued, pointing at the slip. "You can read it right there."

"I had a lovely time. Thanks." She patted down her now half-braided silver hair and started for the door.

"I feel like you're not listening."

"Indeed," she replied, slipping out and heading across the hall. Fishing the key out of her pocket she slipped it into the mechanism, but the door was already unlocked. Inside, Autumn was on the bed, sleeping in her underclothes, her tail flicking much like a cat's.

At least the girl wouldn't see her like this, but they'd have to talk about the door. She'd forgotten to lock it. In any case, she needed to rest. Tomorrow she would go hunting.

CHAPTER VI

Autumn writhed in her sleep, an annoying shuffling sound waking her. As her vision slowly cleared, she saw Zilzina dressed and fitting her weapons into her belt and coat.

"You came back really late last night," the cambion groaned.

"Sorry, it took longer than I expected," answered the elf.

Whatever that means, Autumn thought. "Where are you going?"

"I have to hunt a demon."

Autumn considered the response for a few moments, sleep still clouding her mind. "It's too early for that."

"Go back to sleep," Zilzina said, a softness edging her generally cold tone. "Shit, I still need silver bullets."

"Won't it be dangerous without them?" asked Autumn, suddenly alert and sitting up.

"I can handle it. Don't worry."

"But you don't have to," the girl replied. She shifted to give Zilzina a spot to sit on the bed beside her. "What if something bad does happen?"

The hunter sighed and sat down on the bed. Her silver hair was in a ponytail, as was her fashion when hunting, and her violet eyes shone stark amidst alabaster skin. Autumn noticed she seemed strange, maybe paler than usual.

"This is what I do, Autumn. I know we've only been together for a few weeks, but I've been a hunter for years." She smoothed the girl's hair, a comforting act she'd loved when Serah did it to her as a girl. "And I need to hunt–for more than the money. Not to mention that Serah depends on me to bring money back for her and the children."

Of course, she'll be okay, what was I thinking? Still, Autumn couldn't shake the feeling something bad was going to happen. "What if it's a higher demon?"

Zilzina couldn't help but smile. She ruffled Autumn's hair, which she had just smoothed, and stood. "I'll be fine. Promise." Doing a final check of her weapons, the hunter strode toward the door. "Please stay here. I'll make sure you have plenty of food delivered."

"Okay," said Autumn, feeling a twinge of guilt for leaving the room the night before. She picked up one of the books she hadn't read yet.

"We'll leave when I get back."

"Yay." The girl's tone was sarcastic.

"I won't be long." Zilzina pulled her hood up and slipped through the door, locking it behind her.

Autumn fell back in the bed and sighed. As usual, she was tired, though this time she at least had an excuse. When Zilzina had returned she'd woken, and though she always felt comfortable and safe when they shared a bed, she hadn't been able to fall back to sleep for some time. And now that there wasn't anything to do but wait for Zilzina to return, she knew there was no way she could sleep.

**

Zilzina walked into the shop of the town's only weapons supplier–there was unfortunately no silversmith to be found. She was sorely in need of silvered ammunition. The shop was old, run down, but held a certain ruggedness that the hunter enjoyed, a testament to the tests of time it had withstood. A kind old man who had, at first, been nervous of her appearance had directed her here, saving her from walking the streets aimlessly.

"Can I help you?" asked the large oni behind the counter as she entered. A small chime at the door had alerted him to her presence, though he did not look up from his accounts book.

"I'm looking for silvered 8mm rounds, prepacked if you've got them or can make them," Zilzina answered, setting her ivory-handled pistol on the table. It was an old model, and the tri-barrel configuration was uncommon, but firearms were expensive. And she wouldn't have traded the weapon for anything–it held a number of useful secrets.

The oni held a small lens to its eye and sized up the weapon. "You a hunter or somethin'?"

"I am."

"Huh," he mused, lowering the lens and looking at Zilzina for the first time. "Well, you won't find any silver bullets here. Best bet is to head into the city."

"Really?" Zilzina sighed. She holstered the pistol and stretched her neck. "What about a silversmith? I can work with ball and powder."

"Sorry, your trade ain't much plied in these parts. Probably have better luck in the outer regions if you're not keen on Sapoul. Silver's in short enough supply as it is." The oni looked back to his accounts as he spoke. "Mind me askin' what bounty you're chasin'?"

Zilzina slipped the bounty poster out of her jacket and slid it across the counter. The oni glanced up at it.

"Ah, that one," he said. With a clap, he closed the dusty accounts book and stood. "Well, I may not have silver, but I do have an idea where you can start lookin'."

"And where's that?" asked Zilzina. Her natural suspicion was roused, though she didn't sense any enmity from the oni.

"Out on Eucan Road, near the bend north of town. Nice shady spot for a demon to hide," the oni replied, gathering a set of keys and donning an overcoat. He flicked the keys in his hand as he walked toward the front door and locked it.

"And you're going to take me there?"

"If you'd like." Front door locked, the oni was heading past rows of swords and spears toward the back now. "You comin'?"

"Why help me?" Zilzina asked as she followed the shopkeeper outside. There was a small motor vehicle parked in a simple shed, which he unlocked and slipped inside.

"Not many hunters around these days," the oni muttered as he turned the engine over. "Less still 'round these parts. Bounties are all out in the outer regions, though I swear things are getting more dangerous here by the day."

Zilzina followed him and hopped into the passenger seat, not bothering to open the door. The oni smiled somberly at her.

"My son thought he could... Well, no one else was doing anything about it, of course he had to try."

"I see." Zilzina leaned against the side door as they pulled out of the shop. She rarely had the chance to ride in a motor vehicle, but she always loved the feeling of the wind in her hair when the opportunity presented itself.

"Anyway, I'm proud of him for trying," continued the oni

as he pulled out onto a road and accelerated toward the east side of town. "Just kill it, will you?"

"I will."

***

A knock sounded at the door after Autumn had been half-reading, half-dozing for a while. Probably someone with food. Autumn muttered a few select words she'd heard from Zilzina–words that would've made her mother scold her–as she rose from the bed and shuffled over to the door. She brought a blanket with her rather than getting dressed and slipped the mask over her face before opening it.

"Hi!" Gaia bounced happily on the other side, holding a tray with oatmeal and some fruit on it.

"Hi," replied Autumn. She took the tray and looked back at Gaia's beaming face. "Uh… thanks."

"Okay, bye!" Gaia said and ran off down the hallway.

Shaking her head, Autumn set the tray on the bedside table and laid down again. She didn't feel particularly tired, but she must have fallen asleep because the next thing she knew she was waking up to the midday sun streaming in through the window. Zilzina still wasn't back from the hunt.

She regretted being short with Gaia earlier but, like Zilzina said, they weren't staying long. It was better not to make attachments. *That's probably how Zilzina feels about me*, the girl thought as she dug into her now cold breakfast. *She can't become attached since she'll be leaving me in Sapoul.*

Autumn read for a long while and then decided to enjoy the luxuries of their suite and have a bath. There was no need for her to heat water, she simply slipped into cold water and focused her energy on heating it. It made the typically unenjoyable task of preparing a bath much easier, and Zilzina could even use it after her, once the water was warm. Zilzina… Perhaps she'd been harsh in her earlier judgment. The hunter was doing her best.

It's not like she'd asked for a half-demon girl to be put in her care.

Just as she was drying off and dressing again, Autumn heard a knock at the door. It was late afternoon by that time, and she hurried to open it, hoping that Zilzina had lost her key. Still, to be safe, she donned her mask as usual. It was Gaia again.

"Hi," said the innkeeper's daughter. She held her hands behind her back and looked embarrassed.

"Hey," Autumn replied. "Sorry about earlier. I was just tired."

"It's okay." The elf girl brought her hands from behind her back, revealing a plate of cookies. "Your sister left early, and I thought maybe we could have some cookies since she isn't back yet and you might be hungry."

"Oh, thank you." Autumn paused, appraising Gaia who

obviously expected to be invited in. Zilzina would kill her if she knew, but... Gaia would understand. They were friends, weren't they? "I... do you want to come in?"

Gaia nodded excitedly and stepped inside, taking in the room as if she'd never been within before. She noticed the books on the bedside table and rushed over to take a look, setting the plate of cookies down and picking up one of the volumes. "Oh, I like this one. Mother doesn't know but I read it while she is working."

"It's really good, isn't it?" Autumn replied, forgetting her worries in an instant. She walked over by Gaia, picked up a cookie, and lifted her mask slightly to take a bite. "I don't think there's anything better than books."

"Uhm, have you ever been to a play?" asked Gaia. She watched Autumn reset her mask with intense curiosity.

Autumn had never been to a play, though she badly wanted to. "Still doesn't beat a good novel."

"I guess so." Gaia pulled herself up onto the bed and selected a cookie for herself. "My favorite play is The Nightingale's Kiss."

The pair chatted on for some time like this, discussing plays and novels and anything else they could think of. It seemed to Autumn that Gaia also lacked friends her own age, though she interacted with many people in the inn. As the elf girl was pointing out some of her favorite passages in the books her brother had loaned Autumn, the cambion decided to pry a bit. She wanted to know more about the person who'd cracked through Zilzina's cold exterior.

"Your brother really saved us from your dad the other day, you know, and Zilzina seemed to have a good time with him. He's alright," said Autumn.

"My brother?" Gaia asked, a confused tone in her voice.

"Yeah, the red-eyed elf is your brother, isn't he?"

"Oh, yes. He's my brother!" The girl's tone changed and took another bite of her cookie. "He's not around much though."

"I'm sorry," Autumn replied, noting the young elf's sudden shift. Children were strange.

"It's okay, I don't think he's ever really been around much. I can hardly remember him when I was younger. I think he traveled a lot."

Deciding not to press it further, Autumn fidgeted with her mask and looked to the door. *Where is Zilzina?*

"Why do you always wear a mask?" Gaia asked from the bed.

"Oh, uh, I just like to," Autumn lied.

"Do you wear it all the time? Can I try it on?"

"I don't know…"

"Please? We're friends now, and friends share."

Friends… Autumn repeated the word in her head and

couldn't help but smile. *Friends.* She'd only ever really had a few friends: first, her mother, then Zilzina, and Martha and Klaus. That knot formed in her stomach that always appeared when she thought of the dwarves. Yes, Martha and Klaus were her friends. And now they were dead. *What if...* No, this was different.

Gaia was her friend. Things would be okay.

"If you have a scar or something, I promise I don't care," Gaia was saying as thoughts raced through Autumn's mind. "And if you don't want to, it's okay-"

"No," Autumn said emphatically. She put a hand to her mask. "I'm going to take it off." Slowly the cambion removed the covering, revealing first the two small horns protruding from her forehead, then the black eyes and dusky red scales.

As she watched, Gaia's face slowly contorted in horror. She shrank away from Autumn and whimpered, a small, scared sound as she slipped off the bed and edged toward the door. "W- what are you?" the girl asked.

Autumn lowered her head, her stomach dropping. Why did Gaia look so scared? Why was she running? Why did everyone run? "Please don't leave," she whispered.

Gaia stood by the door and flinched when Autumn tried to move closer, thinking better of it when she saw the young elf's reaction. "Please don't hurt me," whimpered Gaia.

It had been naive to think this could have turned out any

way but disastrous. "I won't hurt you," Autumn replied, refastening the mask to her face. "Just... just go. Please don't tell anyone."

"I won't, I promise." Gaia opened the door and slipped through quickly.

Autumn locked the door and leaned heavily against it. *Well, that was stupid*, she thought, cursing her decision. *Why didn't I just listen to Zilzina and read a book?*

Why couldn't the world just accept her? If they just got to know her... And where was Zilzina?

***

"Thanks for the ride," Zilzina called as she vaulted over the low door out of the vehicle. She could already detect the rotting-flesh scent of a demon nearby.

"I would don my mask and follow you if I could," replied the oni sadly. "But that life is behind me."

Zilzina nodded her understanding and drew her dagger. The fiend was close. As the oni pulled away back toward the town, she stealthily ascended a small ridge near the road. With a scent this evident, the demon must have been intentionally not masking it, letting other fiends know that this territory was taken. It must be a strong one.

It wasn't difficult to track the demon's recent movements, and Zilzina knew as soon as she passed several mangled corpses in the forest that she must be getting close to its lair.

The bodies were in varying states of decomposition. None had been fully consumed–the beast was killing for fun, not necessity. There was no doubt about it, this was the d-

It was all Zilzina could do to avoid being hit by two of the demon's four arms as it charged her from behind a nearby tree. Her reflexes just saved her, but this foe was quick. She made a note not to underestimate it. The two fists collided with a small tree trunk, splintering it easily.

This was almost certainly a higher demon.

"You dare challenge me?" the fiend asked. It held its four heavily muscled arms high and beat its chest harshly.

Dagger in hand, Zilzina hunched in a combat stance. She took slow steps, circling her foe and looking for signs of weakness, waiting for the moment to strike. This demon was one of the largest she had ever encountered, with two long horns–a sign of age, and in turn of power–and sickly red eyes standing out against pale yellow skin.

"Are you unfortunate races now so bold?" the fiend sneered.

"You're bold yourself. Don't worry, I'll cut you down to-"

In an instant, the demon charged Zilzina, a blur of pale-yellow driving into her side. The hunter managed to protect her abdomen with crossed arms but was sent crashing through the brush. *Shit, this one was fast*. Way too fast. Before Zilzina could catch her breath, the demon attacked again, slamming a set of intertwined hands down where she had just been as the hunter rolled out of the way. Or at least she thought she did. A second set of hands grabbed her left leg and wrist, the hand holding her silver dagger.

"Impudent elf, I will teach you-" the demon began but stopped short, inhaling deeply. It groaned and closed its eyes. "What is that intoxicating aroma? Whose blood is it? Yours? No, someone else's." It pulled Zilzina closer and looked her in the eye. "I want it. Take me to them."

With a flick of her wrist, Zilzina tossed the dagger to her other hand and slashed the creature's wrist. It let go of her arm and she managed to twist her leg out of its grasp as the beast thrashed wildly at her. Though the demon pursued her, it seemed slow, more sluggish. It wanted her to escape, to lead it back to the source of the scent.

To Autumn.

Zilzina stopped and faced her opponent again. The gash she'd made on one of its wrists was already healing. She hated to admit it, but this may have been more than she could handle.

"You're a little different than the others," mused the fiend, flexing its bulging arms as the wound healed. "Your blood does not smell nearly as good as that other, but you will make a fine meal all the same. If you will not take me to the other, I will just have to find them myself."

"I won't let you," Zilzina hissed. She raised the dagger again and waited for her moment.

"Me? You won't let me?" The demon laughed. "Say what you will, but you will do nothing. You can do nothing."

In another blur of movement, the fiend seemingly appeared behind Zilzina, but the hunter was ready. She anticipated and guessed where the attacks would come from and dodged them deftly. As the demon lunged again, catching her upper arms, she wrapped her legs around its lower arms, pinning them to its side. Then she bit down hard on one of its upper arms, her fangs extending as she did so. A gush of blood burst forth, both disgusting and invigorating her as it always did.

The demon roared, casting her aside. She rolled and brought forth her whip, cracking it in a flourish. With another flick of the wrist, the dark cord wrapped around one of the demon's arms as it blocked the attack. It tore at it with the other three arms, but it did not budge.

"Pull," the hunter commanded, and the whip's runes glowed. It made a creaking sound as the aged leather tightened on her opponent's arm.

"Good idea," roared the beast. It jerked its body backward, pulling Zilzina toward itself.

All according to plan.

As she flew through the air, the hunter drew her pistol and

fired all three barrels as she impacted feet first into the demon's chest. Launching herself from the assailant, Zilzina rolled to her feet and holstered the weapon. That was the last of her ammunition. It better have been worth it.

The blast had connected with the fiend's mouth and head, leaving behind a bloody mess. It roared as best it could and thrashed about the clearing. She had done it. Drawing her dagger again, the hunter-

A two-fisted blow connected with her side as the demon moved faster than it ever had before to attack her. The force of it sent her directly back into a thick trunk. She coughed blood and felt something inside her collapse.

Is this it?

"Did you think you had me? Me? Yulav the Horrendous?" The demon's voice gurgled through its mangled jaw, spurts of dark ichor ejecting from its exposed throat with each syllable.

"I-" Zilzina coughed. "I certainly hoped so." It was getting hard to keep up the tough act. She was hurt badly and in a tough situation.

A gurgling laugh rose in the demon's throat. Its horns and tail seemed to extend as the beast loomed over her. "I credit you for lasting this long, elf."

Run. She had to run if she wanted to live–if she wanted to get back to Autumn. With a grunt of pain, Zilzina managed to stand but the demon was instantly beside her. He batted her away as a cat might a mouse, sending her again crashing through the snow, this time connecting with the hard, jagged surface of a hidden boulder. Something within her audibly snapped.

Pure agony coursed through her being but she was alive. Another blow like that, though, and she wouldn't be. As the fiend stalked toward her slowly, playfully, she unrolled her right sleeve, revealing the dark tattoos beneath. Using black magic was risky on a good day. In her condition, it was just as likely to kill her as save her. But there was no choice left. Wiping some of the blood from her head and applying it to the arm she rose shakily as it began to emit a dark sort of glow.

"Honestly, why do you still resist?" taunted the demon "You're dead, just admit it."

In another blur, the demon attacked again but this time Zilzina was faster. She could feel her insides burning as she dodged and delivered a blow to the fiend's abdomen. This time it was the demon who found itself crashing aside.

"Darkfire," it spat as it regained its footing for another charge.

The hunter knew she couldn't keep this up. The magic was literally eating away at her life force, and she was weak as it was. Spotting her dagger on the ground beside her, Zilzina scooped it up and extended the black flames along its silvered edge. Darkfire was an ancient oni technique, said to have been taught to them by the demons themselves. It was incredibly powerful and incredibly dangerous.

Before the demon could attack again, Zilzina took the offensive, dashing past it and slicing through the wrist of both of its right arms at once. With a howl the demon again thrashed through the clearing, this time making to get away from the elf. Had she the energy, Zilzina would have followed but she was almost entirely spent. Maintaining the darkfire was all she could do.

"I'll pay you back for this," Yulav screamed as she disappeared into the snowy wood, leaving a trail of dark blood behind.

Zilzina wanted nothing more than to fall into the snow, to close her eyes and sleep, perhaps not even to wake up again. But she couldn't. Autumn was counting on her.

Autumn.

She needed to get back to her Autumn–the girl had made her promise that she wouldn't die. Her muscles screamed as she gathered her weapons and started back toward the town. Why hadn't that damned oni stayed around with the motor carriage? No, she couldn't blame him, but it would have been nice all the same.

It was a long and agonizing trek back into the town proper. Zilzina was cold, colder than usual, and probably looked like death. Still, no one helped her. Passersby looked on in various stages of confusion and fear. After what seemed like ages, the inn came into view, its generic sign casting a gently swaying shadow in the electric lamplight.

Zilzina pushed through the door and upstairs, ignoring the stares of patrons. There was an unusual amount of people downstairs for this hour and it seemed like she had interrupted some sort of gathering but the hunter was in no state to care. Leaving a trail of blood as she went, she hurried to their room. Everything else was hazy. She had to get to Autumn.

The door was locked. Of course, she'd asked Autumn to lock it. She fished for the key in her shredded coat. It was slippery in her bloodied hand, but she managed to find the lock and turn it. Opening the door, she collapsed forward.

"Zilzina!" Autumn cried, rushing to her side. The girl's face was a portrait of horror as she took in her friend's injuries.

Helping Zilzina to the bed, Autumn rushed back and bolted the door. Then she set about investigating the elf's wounds. Dagger, pistol, and whip were cast aside as Autumn removed what was left of Zilzina's coat. Normally the hunter would have struggled, but as she was there was no energy to spare for it.

Oh no, this is bad," muttered the cambion as she lifted the

base of Zilzina's blood-soaked shirt.

"Calm down, I'll be fine," Zilzina grunted. Neither of them quite believed it.

"What do you mean you'll be alright? Look at you!" Tears were clouding Autumn's vision, but she steeled herself. It was time for her to stop crying and do something for once. "Did you feed? It wouldn't be this bad if you had."

Zilzina shook her head and turned away. "I told you, I'll be fine."

"Here," the cambion said, rolling up her sleeve. "Drink."

"No," snapped Zilzina. With what energy she had left, she tried to move away from Autumn. The hunger was burning her stomach and the smell of Autumn blood was...

"Don't be stubborn. Drink!"

"No," was all the elf could manage to whisper as the edges of her vision darkened.

Autumn turned and found the silver dagger on the floor. Without a second thought, she sliced a thin gash in her wrist. "Zilzina, drink right now."

It was all the elf could do to stop herself. She clenched the sides of the bed and didn't dare look in Autumn's direction.

"If you don't, you'll die. You promised. Stop being so stubborn and-"

In a rush of bed sheets, Zilzina sat up and sunk her pointed teeth into Autumn's wrist, over the gash. Her violet eyes widened and glowed fiercely. The blood was like fire in her throat, but she couldn't stop. It was incredible. It promised power. She wanted it, needed it. More and more.

After some time, Autumn groaned, snapping Zilzina to her senses. She sat up and wiped her mouth.

"Have you had enough?" the cambion said weakly. Her head bobbed dizzily.

Shit. She shouldn't have taken so much. Her blurred vision was returning and the pounding in her ears was subsiding. The pounding. Someone was pounding on the door.

"We know you're in there, demon scum!" someone was shouting in the hall.

Okay, we have to get out of here. Zilzina didn't know what had happened to turn the inn's patrons against them–perhaps her appearance when she'd returned, or perhaps someone had seen Autumn. It didn't matter. She grabbed the still faint, though conscious, girl and gathered their gear.

"We have to go," she said softly as the pounding intensified. Keys jingled outside, the innkeeper. Opening the window, Zilzina lifted Autumn outside. She felt strong, stronger than ever. Her wounds were already healing. Autumn's blood was incredible…

No time for that now. She climbed out afterward just as the door was being opened. An angry mob burst into the room, wielding knives, sticks, chairs, and anything else they had found along the way. "Demon" some shouted, "witch" screamed others. All bore hate in their eyes.

"Hold on," Zilzina said as she leapt from the roof, Autumn in her arms. They landed smoothly in the alley below. The elf took the full brunt of the impact easily, her legs barely feeling the added weight. There was little time to wonder at this newfound strength, however, as the mob was already rushing downstairs and out through the inn's front door. Shifting Autumn in her arms, Zilzina dashed off down the alleyway.

Where would they go? She might be recovered but she could hardly escape the city unnoticed while carrying Autumn.

"Ah, I see you made it down."

Zilzina halted and spun to face whoever had spoken. Before her stood Whatever, the red-eyed son of the innkeeper. He sat on a small hay cart in one of the side alleys. Drawing her dagger as best she could while holding Autumn, Zilzina glanced back down the way they'd come. The mob was fast approaching but not upon them yet.

"I heard what was brewing back there, nasty stuff," the elf shook his head and hopped down from the cart. "This is Shafar," he continued, indicating the dark-skinned man at the cart's reins.

Shafar inclined his head as the cart's mules stamped in response to their master's name. "Balak kat," he said in a language Zilzina did not understand. "Peridas eton Sapoul."

Sapoul, she knew that one. The mob was closing in. There was no other choice, Zilzina hopped onto the cart and Shafar immediately tugged the reins to get them rolling.

"Why?" the hunter called back to Whatever his name was as they gathered speed down the dark alley.

The innkeeper's son simply smiled and watched them leave.

Shafar flicked the reins again, increasing their speed.

"Who was that?" Autumn murmured in Zilzina's arms.

The hunter sat down and nestled her into a space between two hay bales. "That was the innkeeper's son. He helped us get away."

"No," continued Autumn, her eyes drifting closed. "No, it was... a one-horned demon..."

CHAPTER VII

Autumn dropped down from Shafar's cart with Zilzina's assistance. They had stopped off the road, near a forest track. Dawn was breaking through the trees, washing away some of the stress of the night before.

"Thank you, Shafar," Zilzina said to the man, inclining her head slightly.

The foreign man acknowledged her with a wave, whether he understood or not, and flicked the reins. Shafar's wagon rambled slowly back onto the road toward Sapoul.

Zilzina had insisted that they be let off to enter on their own in case news of the altercation had spread. Not to mention she preferred her privacy, especially with Autumn around, and the city guard were too nosy for her liking. They set off into the forest at a slow pace. Autumn was able to talk now but was still obviously a bit off balance. Zilzina cursed herself silently, again, for taking so much. Autumn's blood had been completely intoxicating. Despite her typical self-control, the elf had lost herself entirely in the fiery plasma. And the way it had made her feel after, the glow, the power...

No, she couldn't think about that now. She could feel the hunger rising up inside her again.

"Where did you say Shafar is from?" Autumn broke the silence as they followed the faint deer track.

"South of Frigia, across the sea," replied the elf coldly. "There is a place called Ahntelek. I have never been before, but his words sounded like those I've heard from traveling merchants."

"Oh," Autumn continued. She was carrying her mask, though it was ready at hand in case they came across anyone. "I'd like to go there. I've heard it's warmer in the south."

"Yes, I've heard that too." Zilzina shivered and rubbed at her arms. She wore only her blood-soaked inner shirt, her own coat having been torn to shreds in the battle the night before.

"Here, take this," said Autumn, slipping her jacket off and offering it.

The hunter didn't even look at her, just marched on ahead. "Put it back on, I'm fine."

"Why are you always so stubborn?" Autumn sighed. "You know I don't get cold."

"Just put it back on please."

Autumn grumbled a "fine" and slipped the covering back on.

They walked on for some time, straight through until evening with only brief rests when Autumn felt too faint. The forest was unusually quiet, and they were unable to find any nuts or berries to eat; however, Zilzina refused to head back to the road to find an inn. It was likely that news of their encounter had spread, and she didn't want to risk another fight. Autumn was hungry and frustrated, though she kept it to herself. There was something odd in Zilzina's demeanor, something extra cold, it seemed, towards her. She was watching the elf build a fire under the dry overhang they had chosen to camp in when it hit her.

"A one-horned demon…"

She'd completely forgotten. Between blacking out, her weakened state, and nearly an entire night and day of travel, the girl was struggling just to walk straight, much less sort out what had happened. The image of the demon flashed again in her mind like a burst of flame, making her jump.

"You okay?" Zilzina asked, eyeing her curiously.

Autumn nodded and sat down across the fire from her. "Are you mad at me?"

"No."

"Are you sure? I didn't mean to-"

"I'm not mad at you."

"Okay." Autumn watched as the elf busied herself with inspecting and cleaning her pistol, though she had no ammunition for it.

"I didn't mean to-"

"You didn't do anything," Zilzina interjected before the girl could finish. The polishing grew faster.

"Anyone would have been fooled. I didn't sense him either. It was like he wanted me to see."

"Autumn, I don't want to talk about it."

"I-"

"Autumn!" Zilzina stopped cleaning the weapon and glared at her.

The cambion swallowed. "You know who it is, don't you?"

Zilzina's eyes flared up, their violet glow taking on that unnerving quality they had when they'd met. She could feel her pulse quickening and a sick feeling in the pit of her stomach. "Yes. I know him."

"Sann-"

"Don't say that name. Yes, it was Sannazu."

"Right, dangerous for a demon. And anyway, I could have been wrong," Autumn said, pleading with her own memory. "Or I'm sure there are plenty of one-horned demons."

"None powerful enough to completely mask themselves from me."

"Maybe they could have. Yona, I mean the demon disguised as Yona, did."

"Not like this, not that close. I… should've known…" Zilzina laid back, setting the pistol aside.

"Oh… oh!" Realization dawned upon Autumn. She laid back in the other direction and stared up at the overhang. This sucked, she had never seen Zilzina like this. It was like she had just turned off her emotion, emptied herself of all feeling so she wouldn't feel. Autumn imagined it probably helped in dealing with tragedy–she wished briefly that she could do that herself. "I, uh, I think he might have been the attendant at the store. The one who gave me this mask." She held the oni battle mask up and turned it over in her hands. "It's weird, whenever I try to picture the attendant or the innkeeper's son, it's all fuzzy."

"He's masking himself from our memories," Zilzina said. "I'd prefer not to talk, or if you must, at least change the subject."

"Sorry." So that was why Gaia had acted odd about her brother, why she said he was a traveler. Sannazu has the power to change the reality of people's lives. Autumn thought about this for a few minutes, truly intending to drop the subject, but in the end couldn't help herself from asking, "But if it's, you know, him, why did he give me a mask? And why did he help us escape?"

"Why did he do a lot of things? I don't know, Autumn," Zilzina replied bitterly, her voice tense and choked. "He was right in front of me. And instead of killing him, I... I... Damnit, none of this would have happened if-"

"If what?" Autumn sat straight up, feeling rage surging within her. Rage and fire. "If you'd never met me? If you didn't have to take me to Sapoul? Or stay an extra day? Or maybe if I wasn't around, you could have gone after him?"

"So, what if that's how I feel? Maybe it's true," replied the elf dryly.

A wave of heat blasted out from Autumn and retracted. Sparks began rising from the cambion's scales and the edges of her clothes began to smoke. "Well, I can't help what happened to me," the girl shouted. "And, without me, you never even would have known..."

Zilzina propped herself up on her elbows and looked at Autumn, frowning. The girl's horns seemed to have grown and heat waves rippled in the air around her. "You don't know that," she said, sitting all the way up.

"You had all the time in the world to notice. You... you even had sex with him, didn't you?" Autumn regretted saying it even as the words left her mouth. Her inner fire cooled and the sparks winked out. She was just herself again. "Zilzina, I'm sorry. I didn't mea-"

"Don't," the elf said. She stood and flattened her silver

hair, which was frizzing slightly in the heat that Autumn had radiated. Her face was smooth, calm, no longer filled with anger. All that remained was a cold indifference. "I would have been better off without you."

The words hung in the air between them. Autumn didn't argue–she knew it was true. She met Zilzina's gaze. The elf looked like she wanted to say something else, a softness passed over her features, but she remained silent.

Autumn stood and started to walk away. There really was no one, no place, in this world for her.

"Where are you going?" asked Zilzina, not moving.

"Anywhere you aren't," Autumn called back.

"That's not safe for you."

"What do you care? You can drop the big sister act."

The hunter took a step forward but paused. "You know what, fine. Get yourself killed for all I care." She returned to the fire and looked away.

Autumn kept walking deep into the forest. She hadn't even realized when she began crying but the sound of her tears sizzled in the snow at decreasing intervals. The ringing in her ears grew with her deteriorating state until she couldn't even think straight. She just kept walking and walking and walking.

It wasn't her fault that Zilzina couldn't get Sannazu. The elf wouldn't even have known the demon was there if it hadn't been for Autumn.

No, she hadn't done anything wrong. Nothing. She didn't do… anything.

Autumn fell to her knees and put her hands over her face. The tears streamed freely now. *Why did I say those things to Zilzina? The one person who gave a damn about me and I ruined it. So what if she's upset? Maybe Zilzina is right. I am a burden,* Autumn thought. *If it weren't for me, Zilzina would be off on her quest to avenge her parents and lift her curse.*

Maybe leaving is for the best. Zilzina will be happy to be free of the burden.

Autumn lowered her hands and looked around the darkening wood. She was definitely lost. How had she walked the whole day away? Another great decision in a string of excellent decisions. No use fretting about it though. Autumn rose and started walking again. Her stomach was growling with hunger. Hopefully there was something to eat.

The evening sky dipped further into night. The girl cursed, a word her mother wouldn't have approved of, but Zilzina used frequently. If only her part-demon nature came with the ability to see in the dark. That would've been too convenient. Autumn started gathering what dry kindling she could and tried to remember how Zilzina had started fires. The elf had used a kit with flint and steel. Despite her best efforts, Autumn couldn't summon her inner flame. She was doomed to sit alone in the dark. Night came with a host of sounds that hadn't been so bad when Zilzina was around, but now that Autumn was alone, she jumped at every rustle and snap.

The flashlight Zilzina had given her the night they met would have come in handy about now. She wasn't sure when, but she'd lost it sometime along their journey. That was the night she'd first seen Zilzina feeding. The night Zilzina had pointed her pistol at her. The night she had come after her and saved her.

Autumn wished Zilzina was after her now.

No, there was no great elf hunter coming to save her this time. Autumn had to learn to look after herself. The full moon was high enough in the sky now that she could see a bit, so the girl decided to continue walking. There was really no better option. She didn't, however, see the thin branch in her path until it was too late. It caught and sliced her cheek.

"Shit," Autumn hissed, feeling the thin line of blood. It was just a small cut. She wouldn't die from that.

***

Zilzina sat on a rock, staring at the ashes of the fire that had long since gone out. She was cold. Very cold. But she just sat there, unable to move and feeling sick to her stomach about how she'd treated Autumn.

She wasn't even angry anymore. She was sad, sure, and disappointed in herself, but she was beyond feeling anger.

Sannazu was there. Right there. The demon I have spent years looking for was right in front of me and I didn't even notice. Instead, I...

Bile rose in the back of Zilzina's throat. How could she get him to lift her curse if she couldn't even notice him? How could she pay him back for murdering her parents? A demon who could mask his presence more effectively than anything she'd ever seen, significantly better than the fiend at the orphanage.

How does one kill something that can even tamper with memories, the reality, of others?

She'd spent years chasing a demon who could do these things. Had he been watching her this whole time? Was she just entertainment for him? And why the hell had he helped her and Autumn escape?

It doesn't make any sense. The last time Zilzina had felt this lost was when she'd lost her parents as a child. She'd wandered aimlessly for weeks afterward, there had been no one to help back then–no one until Serah.

Blood. Zilzina shot to her feet and felt a vein stand out on her neck. She smelled Autumn's blood.

Autumn. Shit, why had she let her go? How could I have been so stupid and selfish? The girl was her responsibility, like it or not. She didn't have time to be selfish. Autumn didn't deserve that. She needed to be for the girl what Serah had been to her, at least until they got to Sapoul. She had been too wrapped up in feelings of regret and powerlessness that she poured her anger out on a girl who didn't deserve it. Especially not this girl, who had enough to deal with as it was.

Zilzina drew her dagger and dashed off immediately in the direction Autumn had gone. Either the cambion had hurt herself or... Or something bad had found her. She couldn't think about that right now. If Zilzina could smell Autumn's blood, demons and devils sure as hell could, and they would be rushing toward her as fast as they could.

Faster. She had to go faster.

It reminded her of the first time she'd met Autumn. She'd been chasing a lesser devil that was terrorizing a settlement– the same hamlet where a group of oni and orcs had attacked them upon seeing the cambion. That had been a close call, but she'd made it in time.

Nothing would stop her from making it this time either.

There was a rustling off to her right. A devil was leaping through the forest on all fours. It croaked loudly, answered shortly by another croaking roar from off to Zilzina's left. There were at least two devils headed in Autumn's direction already, and that's just what Zilzina could see. How were there so many this close to Sapoul? She knew things were getting worse, but this was bad. There should have been patrols of Frigian soldiers taking care of hellspawn in such high population areas like this.

The situation was bad. Very bad. The scent of Autumn's blood had grown in strength even since Zilzina had met her. What made it so powerful? So... desirable? A mystery for another time. Zilzina didn't dare risk using her dark magic even after the rejuvenation of Autumn's blood–it could kill her outright to use it too often.

She would have to save Autumn the old-fashioned way. Slicing through one devil at a time.

Her whip snapped at the devil to her right, wrapping around one of its limbs and yanking it out of the trees. She made sloppy work of its neck with her dagger, but this was no time to get surgical. Its blood sprayed across her features, exacerbating what was already a terrifying visage as her bloodlust kicked in.

The devil to Zilzina's left leapt at her, sensing the danger in its vicinity. The hunter was quick, however, and snapped her whip at it in midair. The devil managed to catch the leather thong but with a word, "wrap," Zilzina commanded the enchanted weapon to subdue her foe. The fiend was taken by surprise and by the time it was struggling out of the bonds Zilzina was upon it, slitting its throat hastily.

"I'm coming Autumn," she whispered, setting off again toward the cambion's fiery scent alongside who knew how many demons.

***

Autumn could hardly continue walking. Her legs threatened to give out under her. She was starving and tired and scared.

It had been almost an entire day since she'd left Zilzina. There had to be a town or village somewhere. Even if she didn't have any coin, there was always theft. Desperate times and all that. Or perhaps there was a berry bush or a stream to catch fish. Zilzina had shown her how. But she hadn't seen or smelled anything.

There was a shifting sound behind her. The girl whirled around but no one was there. No one and nothing, save for the rotting smell of a demon. Autumn knew she had no chance of fighting the beast off. She broke into a sprint, unsure of where she was going but knowing that she had to get away.

The rustling sounds grew louder and more frequent, now accompanied by croaking roars. Autumn called on a last burst of energy. She didn't want to be eaten–her last memories of her mother were of her cries of pain while her... father gnawed on. She had still been alive at the time. No, she wouldn't go like that.

Autumn ran as fast as she could, not daring to turn back. The pursuit grew closer, and she could hear what sounded like galloping and heavy panting. Her own breath was coming now in ragged pants. Something scraped against her arm, and she screamed. A wave of flame emanated from her, sending the devil that was on her heels crashing into a tree. She glanced back and saw the fiend get up and shake the blow off.

She couldn't slow down. Her muscles were burning with effort. How long could she keep this up? There were at least two fiends in pursuit now. What was going on? Why were there so many?

Her blood. Autumn had lived her whole life alone with her mother, mostly in the woods–there had been plenty of injuries, but nothing like this had ever happened. Perhaps her mother had precautions she never noticed, or perhaps the blood's draw was getting stronger for some reason. She'd seen how the devil, her father, had desired it, not to mention Zilzina's weakness for it.

A heavy blow landed on her side, sending the cambion sprawling into the snow. A dark-scaled beast knelt above her triumphantly. As it opened its maw to bite her, Autumn quickly brought her oni mask forward and lodged it between its fangs. It was strong enough but only just. Already cracks were forming in the ceramic as she fended off the devil's advance, not to mention the other fiends quickly approaching.

This is it. I left Zilzina and this is the price. They'll bleed me dry and tear me to pieces.

The devil above her continued to push. She could feel its

hot breath streaming through the eyes and nostrils of the face covering. Suddenly, the mask shot up, as if a heavy weight was removed from the top. The devil that had been atop Autumn disappeared, replaced by Zilzina, breathing raggedly, and holding her bloodied dagger in one hand and the glowing whip in the other.

"Get up, we have to go."

The cambion scrambled to her feet as Zilzina engaged another approaching devil. The hunter threw her silvered dagger to catch another monster in the throat then turned back to her own foe and used the whip to snap its neck, giving her time to roll over and retrieve the knife. With a practical flourish, the elf carved a deep gash into the injured devil, its head lolling on a broken neck as Autumn ran past.

"Zilzina, I'm so sorry," Autumn huffed as the elf fell into step behind her. "I should never have-"

"Nor I, but now is not the time," replied the elf grimly. More pursuers crashed through the underbrush after them. "Just know that you are not a burden."

They continued on through the forest for some time, Zilzina's keen night-vision guiding them. It was impossible to tell how many demons and devils were after them. Far too many for Zilzina alone. They entered a large clearing and slid to a stop as hideous monsters appeared from the trees around them in all directions. Had they been herded here? A large, flat stone sat atop a small rise in the middle of the clearing. It was only too perfect a place to die.

"Why are there so many?" Autumn panted. "Do they not threaten the surrounding people?"

"It is strange," muttered Zilzina. She guided Autumn toward the center of the clearing, toward the flat stone–it might as well have been an altar. "Hellspawn can't stand each other. They'd never coordinate like this unless there was a higher demon forcing them to."

As if on cue, a shadow passed across them, eliciting a shiver. The lesser devils stopped approaching as the large, bulbous form of their master settled down lazily onto the central stone. "My, my," purred the yellow horror. "Just what is that sumptuous scent?"

CHAPTER VIII

Zilzina pushed Autumn behind her, an instinctive move, and likely a useless one given the situation, but it made the girl feel better all the same. At least they were back together. The enormous demon before them emanated power. Even Yulav had not approached this level. The only other creature Zilzina knew of that could inspire this type of awe was Sannazu. Was this fiend on his level? No, he was unique.

She wouldn't die here. There was still revenge to be had.

"In my many, many years," purred the yellow demon as she tucked her large wings in and lounged on the table. "I have never known one such as you." She extended one of her four scaled arms in Autumn's direction.

"Listen, Autumn," Zilzina whispered, drawing the girl close. "I'm out of silver bullets and using magic will be risky. Be ready to move when I say so."

Autumn nodded. Her muscles tightened in anticipation, ready to spring.

The demon cocked her head. "What's this about running? I'm afraid I've had enough of chasing for tonight."

In a blur, the demon's bulbous form shifted right in front of them. Zilzina hadn't even had time to raise her whip, as she intended. She was locked in the creature's gaze, entranced by the foul power within those dark eyes. It wasn't so much magic as an aura of fear, both natural and unnatural. It washed over the elf and the cambion, as did the fiend's noxious odor, carried on the gust of wind from her wings that had propelled and stopped her so quickly.

The demon squinted at Zilzina and smiled. "Impressive, there is strength in your blood," she said and shifted her gaze to Autumn. "And there is pleasure in yours. What a strange pair you make. I am glad to have crossed your path. I assume it was you who put Yulav in her place?" Flexing her four arms, the demon started to circle Zilzina and Autumn, the nearest devils retreating farther as she crossed between them and the edge of the ring. "Yulav the Horrendous, what a joke."

Zilzina tensed, looking for an out but coming up with nothing. She had to do something. Autumn rotated behind her as the demon circled them like prey. At last, she pulled up her sleeve and started to bite her thumb in preparation to cast a spell when the demon spoke again.

"Too bad I have bloated myself on that village." The enormous beast yawned and extended her wings. With a few powerful gusts, she rose into the air and hovered lazily. "I wish to sleep. You are a treat best enjoyed on an empty stomach."

Zilzina didn't believe in luck, but she was willing to take this one. She had no idea how they would deal with this creature, but Autumn would be safe in Sapoul. No demon, not even one of the higher order, would dare operate within the city limits. The rest they would figure out later.

The demon inhaled deeply. "Ah yes, it was you who engaged that fool, Yulav. And, what's this?" She sniffed the air. "Ah, Sannazu as well? My, my. You two will be a treat!"

Zilzina's eyes widened at the words. *How can she say his name?* The elf cracked her whip and commanded it to wrap around the hovering demon's leg. "You're the first hellspawn I've met who could utter his name. Tell me everything you know about Sannazu."

The yellow demon eyed the glowing whip cord wrapped around her leg mildly. With a soft brush of one of her lower hands it fell to the ground, the magical glow disappearing. "Rubbish," she purred and slipped closer to Zilzina and Autumn. "What do you take me for? Filth, like them?" She jerked her large head toward the cowering devils. "And you, well... you do have Sannazu written all over you. I'll savor robbing him of his pet."

"I'm no one's pet," Zilzina shouted, wishing she had ammunition.

"We shall see," replied the demon with a grin. She turned her bloated form and began flying away, the devils retreating to the forest at a wave of her hand. "You have fire in your eyes, elf. Stay alive until the next time you meet Nyxx. I will come for you both."

What had just happened? They were alive, but why? Nyxx. She was strong. She could say Sannazu's name. Zilzina's head was spinning but she had more important things to take care of right now.

"Are you okay?" the elf said, turning to Autumn.

Without a word, the girl rushed forward and hugged Zilzina. "I'm so sorry. This is all my f-"

"Hush, none of that," Zilzina interjected, returning the hug. "None of this is your fault. Everything is okay now. Let's get you to Serah's, okay?"

"Okay. Thank you." She followed as Zilzina led the way across the clearing that had been encircled with devils but moments before. "But, Zilzina?"

"Yes?"

"I'm hungry."

Zilzina smiled and then couldn't help but laugh. A higher demon had threatened them and would be coming back, there was an influx of hellspawn in populated regions, and they were in pretty bad shape, but somehow, she couldn't stifle the laughter. Autumn joined in as well. It was all they could do in the face of what they'd just overcome.

"Okay, okay," Zilzina answered when she'd recovered enough to speak. "We'll find something."

**

"Welcome to Sapoul," Zilzina said as they broke through the tree line to view the sprawling city. District upon district of multi-levelled apartments squatted below a large clocktower, once the pride of the Frigian empire. Now, Sapoul was a smog laden shadow of its former self, still the center of industry, but suffering from corruption and inequality. Crowds of people filled its streets, from the poor and homeless to the machinists and merchants who made Sapoul tick. Even from this distance, Zilzina could smell the familiar oil and sweat stench that wafted through the city streets.

This was home and it had been too long since she'd last visited.

"Finally!" Autumn piped up. She looked across the cramped streets with awe. "It's so... so... dirty. How does anyone live here?"

Zilzina laughed and handed the girl back her coat, which she'd been wearing. "They just do. You'll get used to it. Now put this on, cover up."

"It feels so surreal," Autumn said as she put on her coat. Once she had affixed her mask, now sporting a thick crack through the middle, they continued onward. "We're finally here. It feels like we've been on the road forever."

"Well, we made a lot of stops." The elf flashed Autumn an accusatory look.

Autumn was too distracted with the sights to be angry. Her head snapped here and there, taking in mechanics shops and dank parlors, hawking merchants and sulking urchins, motor vehicles and strange beasts. If Miesot was the crown jewel of Frigia, Sapoul was the melting pot. There were people of every race the girl had ever heard, and a number from races she hadn't. Everything was crowded and hot and noisy. Even with her strange getup, Autumn didn't stand out here.

Zilzina led the way through the familiar streets. On one corner, an elderly human was performing petty magic for a small crowd. He pulled a purple flower from thin air and handed it to a young woman in a bustle, drawing scattered claps from the onlookers. A few people tossed copper pennies into his hat as he passed it around and hurried on his way. Moments later the flower vanished, much to the woman's dismay.

"Never trust the street mages," Zilzina warned. "They'll just as soon lift your purse as give you a rose. Look."

Autumn watched as the woman began to panic, realizing

that her own purse was missing. She looked totally out of place among the rough people lining the streets. Her valet, who wore a velvet suit, was assuring her that the brigand mage would be apprehended. Obviously, these people were higher class and judging by their clothes, they wouldn't miss the money. All the same, Autumn felt a bit bad for them.

"Are there others like us here?" Autumn asked as they continued on. She was watching a group of orc children play.

"Sort of," Zilzina replied. "There are all types here, though you and I are pretty unique. Keep your mask tight just in case, and we'll need to get you a breather. Serah may have a spare. The fumes can hurt your lungs over time. Ah, over here." Zilzina grabbed Autumn's hand and led her over to a small bakery. "I've been dreaming of the sweetbread for months."

They paid the young woman at the counter and each took a piece of the incredible smelling sweetbread. Despite her generally cold demeanor, Zilzina looked genuinely happy for the first time in a long time, perhaps for the first time since Autumn had met her. They ate their bread and strolled leisurely through the crowded streets toward Serah's.

"So, about the demon, Ny-," Autumn said after she'd finished her bread. She paused on Nyxx's name, glancing at Zilzina just in case, then continued "Nyxx. She could say his name. And, apparently, I can say hers."

"Yeah. My only guess is she's too powerful to be influenced

by his curses," mused Zilzina, still nibbling at her own bread. She tore off a small piece and handed it to Autumn, who accepted gratefully, pushing it up under her mask to eat. "And Sannazu is the only higher demon I'm aware of powerful enough to have a curse associated with his own name."

"And she let us live."

"So did Sannazu. Things just keep getting... weirder."

***

"There it is," Zilzina said, pointing ahead.

Autumn stared nervously at the big, crooked building the elf called home as they approached. It was set a bit apart from the more populated parts of Sapoul, situated right on the edge of a warehouse district. The lack of crowds led to a quietness punctuated only by the regular puffing of steam tubes beneath the street and the occasional whistle of a passing trolley. The whole scene was serene in comparison to the rest of the city, which seemed dirty and aged.

An enormous oni, large even for his race, stood guard outside the building's front door, his hand resting on the hilt of a curved sword. As they approached, Autumn could see he wore a battle mask like hers, though the oni's was of a darker base material and sported yellow designs.

"Are we safe?" Autumn whispered.

"Relax," replied Zilzina quietly. "That mask is what protects the orphanage, much like yours protects you."

Autumn's hand went to the crack in her own mask as the oni appraised them, his practiced eyes sizing up the cambion and the elf. With a grunt, he stood fully–he'd been leaning on the wall before–and crossed his arms. "Do I know you?" His voice was a deep grinding that carried despite low volume.

"I hope so," Zilzina chided with a smile in her voice as she lowered her hood. "Unless your memory is going in your old age, Grymble."

The oni, Grymble, squinted. "Ah, our little Zilzina, come home to pay her respects," he said and relaxed. "Though it would seem that respect does not extend to her old friend. My eyes aren't what they used to be."

"You wound me, ancient one." Autumn had never seen Zilzina this playful. "I ignore or slay those I don't respect. Insults are reserved for friends."

"Indeed. Lucky us." Grymble turned toward Autumn. "And who might this be? An oni warrior come to join us?"

"This is Autumn," replied Zilzina, putting a comforting hand on the girl's shoulder. "As for the mask, well…" She nodded. "Show him."

Hesitantly, Autumn lowered her hood and slipped the mask off. She waited with bated breath as the oni looked her up and down, waiting for him to react with disgust. Instead, Grymble just grunted.

"I'll let Serah handle this one," he said and turned to open the door for them. "It is good to see you, little elf."

"It's good to see you too. We'll catch up later," Zilzina said as she guided Autumn in.

The inside was warm and smaller than Autumn had thought, judging by the building's exterior. They were in what appeared to be a common room, with tables and chairs and sparse decorations. Even though Diona's home had been much more extravagantly outfitted, Autumn could already tell they shared a number of similarities: for one, there were toys scattered around and cases filled with children's books along the walls. Also, the sound of tiny, pounding feet was evident from upstairs and, the warm smell of home-cooked food wafted in from the kitchen in the back.

There was another similarity to Diona's: Zilzina was beaming.

As they stood there, a dwarf girl chased a young oni boy down the stairs in the corner, both of them laughing hard. Behind them followed a pair of female half-orcs, perhaps Autumn's age and very similar looking, likely sisters.

"Zilzina!" one of the sisters squealed loudly, instantly drawing an eruption of scrambling sounds from the rest of the house. The two running children stopped and noticed them, and three smiling heads popped out from the kitchen. More and more came tumbling down the stairs, so many that Autumn lost track, soon trapped in a swarm of children from toddlers to young adults.

"You may want to take cover," Zilzina leaned close to Autumn and whispered.

"Zilzina! Zilzina!" It seemed everyone was shouting as Autumn was gently brushed aside. The elf was practically buried beneath an avalanche of children of all shapes, sizes, and colors. As Autumn watched, she noticed a number of half breeds, children with parents of different races that often suffered exclusion from both communities, and children with various injuries or malformations. Even so, none of them seemed to notice, and the elders helped those who needed a hand piling on to their demon hunter sister.

That was what Autumn noticed. They acted like siblings.

"Alright, alright, let's give her some air," an aged, brown-haired human woman said as she entered the room from the kitchen. She cleaned her hands with a towel as she oversaw Zilzina's excavation, her foot tapping in what Autumn first thought was irritation but was actually something more like excitement. Maybe a bit of both. "Well, you took your time coming back," the old woman continued.

"Sorry Serah," Zilzina said as she extricated a particularly clingy young human boy from her leg. "I had an unexpected stop."

"I can see that," the woman, Serah, said. She looked at Autumn, who still wasn't wearing her mask, and tapped her lips thoughtfully. "And what is your name?"

"A- Autumn," replied the cambion bashfully. She was still wary of going maskless in front of others, but so far Serah didn't seem to mind.

"Autumn, what a lovely name," Serah beamed. "Come, let's get you two something to eat." She reached out and took Autumn's hand.

"Coming," replied Zilzina, who was still wrestling playfully with the human boy. "Okay Harriss, we'll play more later." She followed Serah and Autumn into the large kitchen.

Autumn saw now why the front room looked so small. This must be where they spent much of their time, and no wonder with so many mouths to feed. There were cupboards and tables and stoves and firepits. Stirring one of the large soup cauldrons from which the delicious smells emanated was a small, dark-haired boy–shorter than a dwarf and with long, pointed ears like an elf. She'd never seen anyone like him.

"You could wire now and then, you know," quipped Serah as they entered. "You know I worry. We all do."

"Not many telegraphs where I go," Zilzina replied. "But I'll try."

"You always say that." Serah walked over to taste the soup and patted the small boy on the back. "Zilzina, Autumn, please say hello to Otto. He's a gnome."

"Hi," Otto piped up and gave a deep bow. He was standing

on a stool which teetered slightly atop several large books, though he seemed well practiced in keeping it upright.

"Hello Otto, nice to meet you," Zilzina offered as Autumn waved–she was still feeling a bit shy in the energetic new environment.

Everything was happening so fast. She'd been angry at Zilzina for making her come here, pouting and trying to extend their time on the road. Now that they'd made it, she understood. Maybe she could be happy here. Serah was amazing and the children all seemed great. Was it for the best that she stayed? Only one thing would be missing... She watched as Zilzina chatted with Serah and Otto.

The faces of Martha and Klaus flashed in her memory, causing her to step back and knock a wooden bowl off one of the counters. Everyone looked up at her.

"Sorry."

"Don't worry about it," Serah said with a smile. "Otto, why don't you show Autumn upstairs?"

"Okay!" the gnome replied excitedly. He scrambled down from the stool and ran over to Autumn. "This way. Do you like chess? I love chess, we should play. Do you like books?"

Zilzina caught Autumn's eye and winked as the chattering gnome led her out of the room. As they passed through the door back into the chaotic outer room, she mouthed the words "thank you" back to the hunter.

Everything will be okay.

"Her mother?" Serah asked once they were alone.

Zilzina simply shook her head and started chopping a set of vegetables that Serah handed her.

"And the father?" continued Serah, seasoning the soup and tasting it again.

"Dead," the elf replied dryly. "I killed him in front of her."

Sera nodded. "I see. It was good of you to bring her here."

"I couldn't leave her."

"I know."

The two women stood in silence for some time, chopping and seasoning and finishing the meal. Every now and then, a small head poked through the door, but the children knew that they shouldn't interrupt. The tone of the room was serious enough to let them know that.

"You could stay for a while," Serah said at last, her voice catching a bit in her throat.

"It's getting worse, Serah." Zilzina dumped a set of chopped vegetables into the soup and started on some potatoes. "Every day."

"I know, sweetie, I'm sorry," Serah replied. She straightened and looked at her first adopted daughter. "And you know I hate it when you call me that."

"Sorry mom," Zilzina murmured and hugged her.

CHAPTER IX

"Theo, Esha, Audrey, back to the kitchen please. Holmer, I believe Grymble asked for your help outside nearly an hour ago," Serah called out as she left the kitchen. She and Zilzina had just shared a moment and she was not about to let the elf see her tear up in happiness. She had a reputation to maintain.

Serah, still the same as ever, Zilzina thought to herself. There were murmurs of displeasure from the kids as they reentered the kitchen to resume their duties. The hunter bequeathed the knife and chopping block back to Esha and followed Serah out into the common room.

"The grey looks good on you," Zilzina said, drawing an irksome look from her adopted mother. Secretly, she feared the signs of Serah's aging–elves lived much longer than humans and she did not relish the idea of burying her.

"Don't look so sad," Serah replied. "I'm happy to know my

daughter will have a good, long life."

How does the woman always know what I'm thinking? Am I that easy to read? No one else seemed to be able to do it.

"Don't worry, we still have plenty of time." Serah winked at her and started up the stairs.

Damnit, how does she always know? Zilzina followed up the stairs, marveling at how much the house had changed over the years. Serah truly was amazing. She'd devoted her entire life to helping outcast children like Zilzina. The elf had been the first, but over time there had been more. Eventually, she'd been able to buy this place, the orphanage, and the rest was, as they say, history. Serah had practiced magic once, and even still she made a living for all of them by selling charms and potions. That skill had come in handy for managing Zilzina's growing hunger. During those first years, she'd been able to manage it completely with magical elixirs; however, over time, the hunger had grown, and Serah had been unable to quell it. That was when Zilzina began to consider other options.

Serah had never liked that Zilzina became a hunter. She understood why it was necessary and knew there was no better way for her daughter to deal with her unique needs, but still hated it all the same. She'd even helped Zilzina train and had given her the dark magic tattoos–that had been a long argument, but Serah had added a few here and there over time for Zilzina's protection, although she was openly fearful of the toll they would take when used. But Zilzina was strong, stronger than anyone the woman had ever met. Her daughter was a hunter, and she was proud of her.

"A lot has changed since the old days," Zilzina mused aloud as they walked through the upstairs hallway. The sounds of playing and fighting and all the other things children got up to when left to their own devices echoed from the long rooms on either side.

"Yes, a lot has changed, but not too much."

***

"- and then Zilzina went flying through the living room, taking the demon down with one kick!" Autumn was reenacting the battle at Diona's for the other children. After getting over her initial shyness, she was back to her usual, chatty self, and becoming quite the celebrity with tales from the road.

Everyone was on the orphanage's flat roof, having a sort of party to celebrate Zilzina's and Autumn's arrival. There were picnic style tables and benches laden with food and games. It was the most normal thing Autumn had experienced in some time, perhaps ever. Zilzina watched her reenactments and rolled her eyes at the exaggerations, while Serah wore a concerned look and glanced between the two recent arrivals from time to time. Autumn, who was energetically eating and performing at the same time, took no notice–she was very much in the same state as when she'd eagerly shared her story with Martha and Klaus.

Martha and Klaus. Two friends who sadly were not present.

"I threw the knife down the hall and was like 'Zilzinaaa, caaatch!' And then she grabbed it out of the air and plunged it-"

"Okay, Autumn, that's enough for now," Zilzina called out, hiding a smile. Serah had caught her eye with a panicked look. "Less talking, more eating."

"Meh, meh, meh," mocked Autumn, though she did sit down and energetically dig into her remaining food.

"I see she has your aptitude for trouble," Serah laughed. "And attitude toward authority."

"She's a handful," replied Zilzina, taking a bite of an apple. "You'll knock some sense into her."

As they bantered, a dwarf girl and oni boy approached. "I want to go with Zilzina on adventures too," the girl said. "Yeah, I want to kill demons!" added the boy, waving his fork like a trident.

"Zeke, put that fork down before you hurt someone," Serah admonished.

"Killing demons is not the point of my journeys," explained Zilzina somberly. "It's helping people, like

Autumn."

"And you too," Autumn chimed in from her spot across the table. "With your, uh, you know…"

"They know," Zilzina assured her. "Yes, and removing my curse."

"What's a curse?" asked the dwarf girl.

"It's like a sickness. And the only way to get better is to find the one who gave it to me."

"And kill him?" Zeke asked innocently.

Serah gave Zilzina another look. "Okay, that's enough questions for now. Run along," the matron interjected. "You're going to turn my orphanage into a training facility."

"I promise I'm not trying to," sighed the elf. "And I'll talk to Autumn, no more stories."

"No, it's okay. Let her have her fun. Perhaps just less of the gory details."

A loud gong sound reverberated through the air six times, making Autumn jump. "What's that?" she exclaimed with her mouth full, drawing laughter from the children.

"It's the clocktower, silly. It's famous."

"You don't know the clocktower?"

"Everyone knows about that!"

Zilzina opted to sit this one out, allowing Autumn to fend for herself against the barrage of questions. Now she would know what it felt like. She did seem to be thriving in the environment though. It was good for her to be around other children. Leaning back in her chair she whiled away the evening chatting idly with Serah and the children who approached now and then.

"I fear this joy may be short-lived," Serah confided once the sky had darkened and the children were back inside performing their chores.

"Why do you say that?" asked Zilzina, suddenly concerned. She was chewing on a short pipe that Serah had offered her, filled with a certain dried tea that she enjoyed smoking now and then. "These are good times, enjoy them."

The human woman gave her adopted daughter a surprised look. "Well, that's new, coming from you."

"Don't worry, I won't be saying anything that sappy again anytime soon."

"No, no, it's a good change. You've grown, dear. Maybe Autumn has something to do with it?"

Autumn's face, first in fear on the night they'd met, and then in joy earlier that day flashed in Zilzina's mind. "Maybe. Anyway, have you learned anything since I left?"

With a sigh, Serah stood and walked over to the edge of the roof, looking out over the uneven cityscape, punctuated sharply by the Sapoul clocktower, jutting out like a spike. "Their blood, your blood, there are similarities," she said at last.

"You still believe us to be of a unique lineage?" asked Zilzina, walking over beside her and taking a draw from the pipe. Its dying embers flared up, highlighting the elf's violet eyes in the dying light.

"Yes. I'm not sure if Sannazu intended for the curse to cause this exact effect on you. In fact, from what you've told me of Autumn's blood, it's possible that's what he intended for you, but something went wrong. Cambions are not unheard of, but not like her. I'd need to examine her further."

"I see." Zilzina took another drag of the pipe. "She'll be excited to help. Just... give her some time to settle in first."

"Of course." Serah shivered and put a hand on Zilzina's shoulder. "Come on, let's head inside. It's getting cold out here."

"I'll be in shortly."

With an understanding nod, Serah turned to walk inside but paused. "We'll find a way to fix it, don't worry. You and her both. Everything will be okay, you'll see."

"I hope so."

***

Autumn yawned and stretched as the sunlight streaming through the window woke her early the next morning. She was careful to not disturb the human girl, Gina, who was her bedmate, but noticed that she wasn't there. They had set up a wall of pillows between them since Gina complained the cambion was too hot at night, but she didn't mind it too much as long as they didn't touch. The aroma of sausage wafted in through the open door, catching Autumn's attention. She listened closely and her keen ears could hear sizzling from the kitchen.

She was going to like it here.

"Morning Autumn," Esha called as Autumn got out of bed. Her bedmate, Audrey, like Gina, was also missing.

"Morning," Autumn replied to the teenage oni. "Where's Gina and Audrey?" The four of them had been sharing a room for the two days since she and Zilzina had arrived at the orphanage.

"Kitchen duty," yawned Esha. "We'll get you on the rotation soon too."

"Okay! I'm happy to help. And breakfast smells amazing."

"Serah somehow manages to always get us good food. Even when things are tight, the food is always good." Esha slipped into day clothes and led the way through the hall. As they passed doors to other rooms, Autumn spotted the other children waking up and getting ready, the older ones helping the younger. A few of them waved and Autumn found herself unconsciously checking for her mask before smiling and waving back.

They arrived at the shared bathroom, and though Serah had expanded it, Autumn could already tell that it was a major pain-point for the mornings. Zilzina had suggested she simply wake earlier, before the others were using it, but Autumn didn't particularly care for that idea. It was a small price to pay.

A line had formed in the hall, which grew noisier as everyone woke up and started talking and playing. It was slow going but eventually Autumn made it in and washed her face beside Esha. She'd never had indoor plumbing when living with her mother, but ever since hitting the road with Zilzina she'd experienced it at several inns and at Diona's and had no intentions of going back. Hot water on demand was a godsend.

Once washed up and ready for the day, Autumn skipped downstairs. Zilzina was sitting on the couch beside Grymble, each with a different part of the morning paper–the oni guardian appeared to be reading the classifieds and obituaries while Zilzina was scanning through news reports, probably looking for demon activity. Yena and Zeke were playing with a set of blocks on the floor near them.

"Morning, sleepyhead," the elf chimed.

"Not everyone has your freakish morning person... ness," quipped Autumn, jumping down the last four stairs and nearly losing her balance in the process.

"Nor your incredible acrobatic skills and immense vocabulary," Serah interjected as she entered from the kitchen. Autumn had quickly learned where Zilzina got her sarcastic sense of humor from. "How did you sleep?"

"I would say like a baby, but Jan didn't sleep at all, judging by the crying," Autumn replied, though her voice did not carry the tone of complaint. Living with a big family was different but she was getting used to it. "I slept fine though."

"Good to hear," the elder human woman smiled. Autumn thought the streaks of gray made her look regal. She remembered when her mother had found her first gray hairs, making Autumn comb through and pick out every one. "Well, you're just in time for breakfast. And after that I've assigned some chores over to you. Everyone around here pitches in."

Autumn nodded and took her place at one of the tables. Zilzina and Grymble stayed on the couch as the other children filed down and Audrey served each of them plates of sausage, egg, and biscuit. Some of the older children and the adults took coffee, though Autumn couldn't stand its bitter taste. She stuck with juice, leaving the limited milk supply for the younger children.

After breakfast, Serah asked her to mend some hand-me-down dresses, having learned from Zilzina that she was a deft hand with a needle. Autumn wondered how much the hunter had told their now-shared mother about how she knew, thinking back to that night, stitching her up in the boarding room. The cambion took the dresses and a sewing kit up to the roof to work in the sun. It was a nice day after all, plus she liked looking out over the city. She had never been anywhere so busy and open all at once. The wind was still too chilly for anyone but her, so she found the roof a perfect place to be alone for a bit before the day warmed up.

Autumn worked for a while–only an hour in reality, though she told herself it must have been at least three–before taking a break and walking over to lean on the edge of the rooftop balcony when the clocktower chimed nine. Below she saw Grymble at his usual place beside the front door. The oni took his job very seriously and hardly ever left the post, even choosing to sleep in a chair just inside every night. It must have been unbelievably boring, Autumn thought.

"Grymble," called the girl, waving down.

"Reading on the roof again?" the oni grumbled, glancing up.

"Working, Serah gave me chores."

"You don't appear to be working, little one." There was a smile in the oni's voice, though his mask obscured his face.

"Neither do you, but here we are," Autumn chided. Considering the amount of snark from both Serah and Grymble, it was a wonder that Zilzina was not even more difficult, though Autumn did enjoy the banter. "How can you just stand there all day, every day? Don't you get tired?"

"Yes."

"I don't think I could do that." Autumn sighed and looked at her own unfinished chores. "At least not without a break now and then."

"It is my duty."

"Well, obviously, but-"

"It is my duty to stand between this door and the world, to protect the children," Grymble interrupted. "I will gladly do so to my dying day."

A twinge of guilt tugged at Autumn's heart. She hadn't meant to insult the oni. "I'm sorry, I know it's important. I didn't mean to imply otherwise."

"I know. It's okay, little one. Perhaps you'd best be back to your chores."

"Ugh, okay," Autumn complained. "You know, you could at least read a book or something."

Grymble's only reply was a soft hmph as the girl turned to resume her sewing. That lasted another hour or so before she grew bored again and wandered inside. Spotting Audrey in the hall she asked where Zilzina was.

"I'm not sure, probably in Serah's chamber," Audrey replied. "They're always together when she's around, though she hasn't been here this long in some time."

"Thanks," said Autumn, feeling that guilty tug at her heart again. She didn't want Zilzina to leave, even though she knew the elf had to get back out there. Even now she was probably starting to feel the hunger again.

Walking down to the end of the hall to Serah's room, the cambion overheard the pair of women speaking inside. "You plan to leave soon?" That was Serah. Autumn shifted to the slightly open door and saw Zilzina nod.

"As soon as I can," the violet-eyed elf replied. "I can't... wait much longer."

"I thought as much," said Serah. "I just wish you'd visit more often, and, though I know it's too much to ask, stay longer."

"You know my travels take me all across Frigia, even farther sometimes. I promise I visit Sapoul whenever I can." Zilzina paced around the room as Serah brushed her hair at a simple vanity. "Usually there aren't many demons in the area, though what we saw on the road does concern me. I will see about finding Nyxx, I don't like how close she is with the threats she made against Autumn."

A tired sigh escaped Serah's lips. "Please be careful, you've never faced anything like her. A higher demon."

"If I can't defeat Nyxx, I'll never beat Sannazu. I have to do this."

"I know... What about Autumn."

Zilzina paused and looked knowingly to the door, meeting Autumn's gaze. The elf had noticed her immediately, of course, though Serah still seemed unaware. "What about her?"

"She loves you, you know."

Autumn felt her heart sinking as Zilzina looked away, already knowing what she would say.

"I know, but the road is no place for a girl, especially not in the company of a hunter. Do you hear that, Autumn?"

The cambion opened the door bashfully and walked into the room. "Sorry Serah."

"Tsk, you should know better," Serah replied calmly, looking at Autumn in her vanity mirror and continuing to brush her hair.

"So, you plan to leave soon then? Without me?" Autumn could feel herself choking up.

Zilzina, who had suddenly become rather interested in something outside the window, simply nodded. The elf could feel the cambion staring daggers into her back. "That was the plan from the beginning, you know that."

"But you don't have to leave," Autumn pleaded.

"You know that I do."

"You said it yourself, there are more demons here now, or... or..." Pulling her sleeve up, Autumn pointed to her wrist. "I can help!"

"No," Serah and Zilzina said together.

"I can't do that again," Zilzina continued, finally looking back at the girl. "It's too dangerous."

"But-"

"No. Besides, I have to find Sannazu," the elf said. She walked over to Autumn and gave her shoulder a squeeze. "Serah has agreed to help you as well. We'll find out why your blood draws hellspawn like flies. It's best this way, for everyone."

"No one even asked me!" shouted Autumn, pulling away. "You say it's best for everyone but I didn't even get a say. It's not fair!"

"Life isn't fair," Zilzina returned, her own voice rising. "Do you think I want to drink that filth for the rest of my life? It's revolting! I hate it and I hate myself for it!"

A heavy silence fell upon the room and the rest of the house grew quieter. That tugging guilt was now an iron weight tied to Autumn's heart. Of course, Zilzina hated her curse, of course she had to find a way to lift it. *Why am I so selfish?* Autumn thought and lowered her head so the elf wouldn't see her tears.

"I- I have chores to finish," the girl sniffed and slunk out of the room.

***

"That was harsh, even for you," Serah stated. "They may not have been expressed correctly, she's just a girl, but you have to understand her feelings."

Zilzina was still staring at the door. "I know, I do," she

193

replied weakly, her voice raw from holding back her own emotions. "This is the best I can do."

Why did Autumn bring out this side of her? She hated the way it made her feel to disappoint the girl.

"She's not unlike you, you know. I had a hell of a time keeping you here when you were an adolescent." Serah laughed, lost in memory. "You were going to go off and slay Sannazu on your own, your mother's wishes be damned. It breaks my heart every time you leave, but I know you're strong. So is Autumn, she just doesn't know it yet."

"Now I'm being lectured?" Zilzina quipped, feeling the tension break as they reminisced. She sat down next to Serah and pulled her own silver hair into a ponytail. "Just look at what that cambion has caused."

A cough accompanied Serah's chuckle this time.

"Are you alright? You need to have the kids pitch in more, you're working yourself too hard…"

"I'm fine," Serah said. Her voice had that determined tone that Zilzina meant there would be no further discussion on the matter.

"Okay. By the way," Zilzina continued, reaching into her jacket for a purse. "It isn't as much as last time, but I couldn't take as many contracts."

"It will go a long way." Accepting the purse with a hug, Serah stood and stretched. "Ah, maybe I will have the children take on some more of the heavy cleaning. My old bones aren't as strong as they used to be, even with the medicine."

"Speaking of which," Zilzina replied, looking around. "No ingredients or potion bottles. Is business that bad?"

"Far from it." The woman pointed to the vanity's mirror and muttered something under her breath. Within Zilzina now saw a room, the same room though with different furniture, filled with spells, charms, potions, containers, and all other sorts of mystic paraphernalia. Looking back to Serah, the elf realized that they were now in that room, the only remnant of Serah's bedroom set being the vanity, which was now covered in potion-making ingredients instead of toiletries.

In the middle of the room was a long table littered with bottles filled with odd-colored liquids and papers covered in strange symbols. Wooden charms swung here and there on thread and the sickly-sweet cinnamon smell of Serah's favorite incense hung heavy in the air.

"Neat trick, you'll have to teach me that one," Zilzina murmured.

"This one may be a little beyond you, sweetie. Also, it requires one to stay in the same place, not really your style."

Zilzina stuck out her tongue–she'd picked that one up from Autumn–and looked idly through some of the papers.

"Did something happen?"

"No, just an abundance of caution," Serah replied. Pulling a brown paper package out of a cupboard, she inspected the label then returned it. "Some of the religious sects have been stirring up more anti-magic sentiment. I'd rather not risk any issues. Only Grymble and I have access to this room. It's also safer for the children."

"Sounds like you've got everything figured out."

"Well, I do have a small problem," Serah continued, pulling out another package, reading the label and removing it to hand to Zilzina.

"What is it?" the elf asked, glancing at the label. Hansel Gindenverg. "Oh, don't tell me you did business with this thug."

"He ordered a rather potent charm and has refused to pay for over a week now. I'd send Grymble but–and don't tell him I told you this–he's not as young as he used to be."

"I've noticed. Don't worry, I'll get the money." Zilzina walked back over to the vanity and waited patiently.

"Now, Zilzina, there are many ways to solve this problem," said Serah, walking over to the mirror and waving her hand. They were again in her bedroom, the sounds of the house having returned after Zilzina's and Autumn's argument.

"Well, there are at least two: yours and mine," the elf said haughtily, striding towards the door. "You tried yours, now let me try mine."

"I swear you have the hardest of heads."

"You know it. I'll sort this out, I need to pick up more silver bullets anyway."

"I'll leave it to you then."

***

Zilzina knocked on the door to one of the children's rooms and walked in. Inside, Otto, the gnome, was playing chess with Erizeled, one of the younger dwarves.

"Hey guys," Zilzina said, examining the board state. It wasn't pretty. Otto was winning handily.

"Hi Zilzina," Otto chimed.

"I think I hate chess," grumbled Erizeled, drawing a burst of laughter from the gnome.

"It isn't polite to gloat," Zilzina said. She picked up one of the castle pieces and moved it to check Otto's king. "You left your defenses wide open here."

Otto scratched his head and smiled as Erizeled suddenly renewed his interest in the board.

"Anyway, have either of you seen Autumn?"

"No," replied both, returning to their game.

"Are you leaving already," Erizeled asked glumly, noting Zilzina's travel outfit.

"Just running an errand, I'll be back tonight." She ruffled the boy's hair. "But I do leave tomorrow."

"Autumn won't be happy about that," Otto muttered, still deep in thought examining the board. "It's all she talks about."

"I know, that's why I want to find her."

"She's usually on the roof," Otto continued, making a rather clever move, to Erizeled's despair. "Don't worry, when you're gone, we'll take care of her."

"I'm sure you will. Thanks guys."

Zilzina headed up to the roof where Autumn sat, pretending to read a book. The cambion made a show of turning her chair away from the door as the elf walked out.

"Pretty mad, huh?"

"Yup," Autumn snipped, turning a page she hadn't read.

"Well, I have to step out to help Serah with a few things." Zilzina started to approach but thought better of it. "We'll talk later tonight, okay?"

"Don't worry about it." Autumn turned another unread page pointedly. "You're just doing what's best for everyone."

"Yeah," replied Zilzina quietly. With a sudden shooting pain, her hunger flared up, its fierce burn eliciting a groan from the usually stoic hunter. Her senses went into overdrive: the *shh* of Autumn's fingers on the pages, the pulse of her heart, the rush of her blood. The girl didn't understand how difficult it was for them to be near sometimes, how much control Zilzina had to exercise not to just... to just...

Autumn looked up, seeing the veins standing out in Zilzina's neck and the glow in her eyes. "You're hungry, aren't you."

Hunger? Yes, but there was something else, something that had been growing ever since she'd fed on the cambion's blood. It was desire. "I need to head into the city," was all the hunter could manage, turning to leave.

"Let me help you…"

"Not this time, Autumn. I'll see you later."

As Zilzina started to leave, Autumn choked up again, but this time she wasn't angry. "Just promise to come back, okay? Soon."

"As often as I can, promise," Zilzina said, fighting down her hunger and pausing.

"Don't leave me alone again."

"Never."

CHAPTER X

The Foaming Shandy was a human bar in the old city known for its seedy, and generally racist, clientele. Sapoul had its fair share of supremacists despite the diverse nature of its populace. Tensions between various groups sometimes boiled over into violence, with the humans being the worst, though usually things rested just shy of action unless someone stepped over distinct boundary lines.

Zilzina hoped her actions today wouldn't tip that balance.

The elf stepped into the crowded bar, drawing immediate attention. *In and out, just need to find Hansel,* she thought to herself. Shifty eyes followed her the whole way to the bar, the thud of her boots resonating through the now quiet taproom. He was there alright, center of the party, a spherical pendant hanging from a chain on his chest. Cronies leaned in close, whispering to the thug as Zilzina approached, but he waved them away.

"It's a charmed necklace made of redwood," Serah had explained. *"And might I say it was very complicated to-"*

"Only important details please," interjected Zilzina in the nicest tone she could manage.

The older woman shook her head in feigned disappointment and continued. "It grants the wearer a barrier to protect from attacks, but it's limited. If you move slowly, it will do nothing, and it slows down the user as well. Only really practical if you're expecting a knife in the back."

"Perfect for a city thug surrounded by other thugs."

"Exactly."

Zilzina lowered her hood, her long, pointed ears and silver hair immediately drawing a murmur. Many of their eyes glanced instinctively up at the sign over the bar–"Humans Only" it read in neat letters. Hansel smiled at her, his greasy blond hair glinting in the lamplight just below the sign. Someone coughed and as if rehearsed the bar emptied of everyone but Hansel, his five cronies, the barkeep, and Zilzina over the next couple of minutes.

Once they were alone, Hansel motioned to a stool. "Have a seat, my lady," he said, sarcasm dripping from his voice. "It's not often your fragile kind graces us with their presence."

"I can't imagine why," replied Zilzina coolly. She continued her measured pace, boots thumping against the wood floor, and took the stool. "Have anything to drink around here?"

The barkeep looked to Hansel, who nodded, and grabbed a mug to fill at one of the tapped kegs. The hiss of the tap and slosh of the liquid were the only sounds until he slammed the drink down in front of Zilzina, splashing some of the sudsy brew onto her. She flicked him a copper coin and took a long drink, wiping the foam from her lip when she was done.

"Well, that is just horrendous," she said, taking another sip.

Hansel and his cronies burst into laughter. The burly leader slapped her on the back. "Sorry, little lady. Fresh out of sweet wine."

"No problem, I won't be here long." The elf turned to Hansel, who was leaning in close beside her on the bar, his stale breath blowing hot in her face. "I'm here to collect what you owe Serah."

"Serah... Serah..." the man pretended to think, looking to his men who also feigned ignorance. "Sorry, doesn't ring a bell. Happy to give you another kind of deposit though."

"Only thing you'll be depositing is the coin for Serah, in my hand, and maybe I'll let you walk out of here with your depositing faculties intact." Zilzina drained her mug and stood up, resting her hand on her pistol.

"Ah, dios mio," Hansel said, slipping into the southern

tongue. "What a sharp tongue you have." He stood and flexed, nodding to his cronies who formed a semicircle around the elf. "I can think of a better use for i-"

In one swift motion, Zilzina brought her boot up and kicked Hansel square in the jaw, moving slowly enough to pierce the shimmering barrier that appeared around him but powerfully enough to knock him off his feet. The group was stunned, looking from their fallen leader to the elf, who straightened her jacket, cracked her neck, and dared them to attack with a slight beckoning motion.

The stunned Hansel just stared back for a moment and spit a glob of blood on the floor. "Get her."

The group of cronies burst into action, coming at Zilzina from all directions, though their attacks were not well coordinated. Well-practiced in fighting groups of devils, the hunter had no problem dispatching each with non-lethal blows in turn. A spinning heel kick sent one of them crashing face-first into the bar, a few of his teeth clattering across the polished bar top. He would be out for sure. Another pair crashed into each other as she spun out of the way of a lunging third, who was sent reeling with a blow to the stomach and a knee to the chin. The sickening crunch reminded her to be a bit gentler.

Humans were far more fragile than her typical foes.

One by one, they came at her and one by one they fell.

They certainly wouldn't be crossing Serah again. Even if there was some bad blood afterward, the orphanage was so heavily warded that the elf doubted any army could breach it, not to mention Grymble at the door. Once the gang was out of action, she turned back to Hansel, who was watching fearfully from the corner. His eyes darted toward the door, but he knew there was no way he was getting past the enraged hunter quick enough to escape.

"Y- you can't harm me," he said with faltering confidence. "I've still got the charm, see?" He lifted the spherical pendant.

"Yeah?" replied Zilzina, walking up slowly. "How'd that work out last time?"

He took a wide swing at her, which she answered with a measured palm strike to the chest, knocking the thug back into the corner again. *So, this is what passes for strength on the streets of Sapoul these days?* These race gangs garnered power through fear more than anything else. They crumbled in the face of real power. Trying for another swing, Hansel was knocked back again and made a sound that was very... un-thugly.

Zilzina didn't yield. She attacked again and again until the resistance from the shield weakened and eventually gave out altogether. It seemed the charm had its limits.

"I didn't mean anything by it," Hansel whimpered, a bloody mess though not too badly harmed. "I'll pay, I'll pay."

"I know you will," said Zilzina. She shoved him back one more time and held out a hand expectantly. "And I trust you'll remember the lesson for next time?"

Hansel's cronies were slowly getting to their feet, all avoiding eye contact with the elf that had soundly thrashed them. A few had more severe injuries but given their line of work it was simply a hazard of doing business—they'd messed around and promptly found out, in this case.

"I'll pay," Hansel continued. "But I don't have any money now." The withering look Zilzina gave him caused the man to flinch. "Okay, okay, here."

Zilzina didn't wait for him to finish counting out payment from the purse, she just took the whole thing. The late fee would go toward her restocking on silver rounds.

***

Autumn halted outside Serah's room when she noticed the door was open. Inside, the woman was putting Yena and Zeke, the youngest children in the house, to bed although it was still early evening.

"Hello Autumn," Serah said softly without looking up as she laid the dozing Zeke down. "Would you like to join me for a walk? I feel like we've never really had a chance to talk."

"Hi Serah. Okay, sure." The girl thought better of telling Serah that she'd rather go back to reading her book. With the youngest children down, it was the rare time between chores and bed that the house was relatively quiet. One would never imagine the havoc those little creatures were capable of, seeing them curled up in the bed now.

"Like angels now, huh?" said Serah, following Autumn's gaze as she exited the room. "This afternoon more like devils though. The trouble those two get up to." She shook her head.

Autumn stifled a laugh and followed Serah as she walked softly down the hallway. "I'm sorry for eavesdropping the other day," managed the cambion after overthinking a handful of other silence-breakers. "And for saying those things…"

"It's alright. I know it's only because you care for Zilzina. So do I."

The cambion itched the back of her dusky-red scaled hand and looked away. "I'm not sure that matters much to her."

"It matters a lot. More than you know." The older woman sighed. "But her goal has always been very important to her."

"I know, and I understand. I just wish there was more room for… other people."

"If it makes you feel any better, I have never seen my daughter look at anyone the way she looks at you," Serah replied, taking the turn downstairs. "Of course, we are close, but there has always been a… distance. A distance I don't see between you two. You're truly the sister she never had."

"Sister," Autumn repeated to herself. "Thanks Serah, that

does make me feel be-"

The cambion's eyes went wide and she turned to the window, inhaling deeply to be sure she wasn't mistaken. Her heart thudded in her chest.

"Serah."

"Yes dear? What's wrong?"

"Get everyone somewhere safe. Now!"

***

Zilzina was walking down the street toward the orphanage when it hit her: blood. She broke into a sprint, turning the final corner to the front door. Grymble lay motionless on the ground a few yards away, a pool of his blood already congealing in the street around him.

"Grymble?!" shouted the elf, sliding to a stop beside him.

The oni did not stir. Ever since Zilzina had been a child, Grymble had watched over them, standing guard at that door, never failing–and now he was dead. What had happened while she was out? Zilzina closed his eyes when another scent hit her.

Decay. A demon.

Shit. Shit!

There was a demon in the house, or had been. How was that even possible? She wracked her brain, this scent was familiar. She rushed in through the open door, wrenched from its hinges, and was met with a grisly scene. Several of the children had been... she couldn't tell who...

This can't be happening. How did it get into the city?

On the staircase there were more. Theon lay halfway up, crumpled alongside Audrey. Pushing down the need to wretch, Zilzina pushed past them, spotting Otto, the gnome, at the top of the stairs.

"Otto! Where is-" The elf stopped short. Otto was... ceramic. It was obviously him, the right size and shape, a look of horror in his eyes, but, somehow, he was transformed. No time to worry about it now, Zilzina thought, scooping up the ceramic gnome and barreling down the hall toward Serah's room. There were claw marks and some blood but luckily no more bodies.

"Serah? Autumn?" she called out fearfully.

A crying moan came out from Serah's room. Rushing inside, Zilzina saw Esha curled up in the corner near the door, rocking back and forth. As soon as she saw Zilzina, the orc girl grabbed her leg and buried her face. She pointed across the room, to the vanity, where Serah lay motionless.

"Oh, no, no, no," Zilzina repeated, wresting her leg gently from Esha and giving her Otto to hug. "Be very careful with him, okay? That's Otto."

The girl nodded and wrapped her arms tight around the ceramic gnome.

Children secured, Zilzina rushed over to Serah. "Please,

just… no," she breathed, taking in the gash on her mother's stomach. Blood was starting to pool, though it was much less than the puddle beneath Grymble. Tears stung her eyes and blurred her vision, drawing a frustrated grunt from the hunter as she tore a length of cloth from the drapes and pressed it to Serah's wound. "Don't you dare die on me," she said through gritted teeth.

"Zilzina?" asked the old woman weakly. She lifted her now frail palm up to the elf's cheek in what was either a caress or a slap, it was hard to tell in her state. "Get yourself together."

Zilzina blinked and took a deep, calming breath. "What happened?"

"Four-armed demon," Serah panted, straining to sit up against the vanity and looking up at the mirror. "Looking for Autumn. I got everyone I could inside but some… and she took her. She took Autumn."

Yulav. Zilzina's hands formed into a tight fist. That hellspawn bastard had followed them into the city. "You did good, Serah," said the elf. She looked into the mirror. "Okay, we need to get you and Esha inside. Is anyone else out here? I'll take a look."

Serah nodded and accepted Zilzina's assistance in standing, beckoning to Esha. "Come here honey, it's alright now." Taking the orc girl's hand, Serah turned and looked her older daughter up and down. "If you find anyone, bring them here.

Then go save Autumn. We will be okay until you return, I have healing salves and food inside."

Without another word, Zilzina gave her mother and Esha a quick hug and dashed off through the house, checking every room as quickly as she could. There were no other survivors, though luckily it seemed that Serah had been able to save most of the children. *Most...* It felt like such a dirty thought, as if their lives were nothing but a math problem. A philosophical conundrum for another time–for now at least those who lived were safe. With one last look at the carnage Yulav had wrought in the front room, Zilzina ran out the door, past Grymble's body, and out to find Autumn.

Now that she knew what she was looking for, the demon's scent was clear. She followed it as best she could through the twisting alleyways. Before long it was clear where the beast had gone: the clocktower.

Making her way through the winding streets and alleys, Zilzina pushed herself as fast as she could go. With a final leap over an overturned market stall, she finally made it to the clocktower's front entrance. The street was surprisingly abandoned, likely because someone had seen Yulav arrive. The elf drew her pistol, took a deep breath, and kicked in the boarded-over door. Dust puffed up from each creaking step as she dashed up the spiraling staircase to the tower's peak. The ascent felt like an eternity. Each moment could be Autumn's last.

"Ah, I've been expecting you," Yulav sighed as Zilzina finally entered the clock room. The four-armed demon's large frame was silhouetted by weak light streaming in through the enormous, translucent clock face.

"Zilzina," called Autumn from the corner across the room, her voice a whimper of fear and pain.

Zilzina scowled as she caught sight of Autumn, the girl's leg mangled, keeping her in place. The hunter approached Autumn cautiously to check on her, watching the demon the entire time, although Yulav seemed to have no intention of stopping her. The leg was obviously broken, the bone protruding from Autumn's shin was shiny with blood.

Even the cambion's impressive self-healing may not be enough to totally fix an injury that bad.

"I had to keep her still," continued the demon, yawning as if bored. "She kept whining and trying to run."

Zilzina ignored Yulav and put a hand on Autumn's shoulder looking her in the eyes. The girl was putting on a brave face, holding back tears though hot steam was leaking from her tear ducts. "Are you okay?"

"It hurts," Autumn whined. "But I'm okay."

"We'll get you fixed up, don't worry."

"Not that. Serah… the children… because of me…" It took all of Autumn's effort not to break down.

Lost for words, Zilzina simply put a hand to Autumn's cheek. The scales there were hot, much warmer than normal. She had seen Autumn use her inner fire before, but as smoke took the place of the steam leaking from the girl's tear ducts, Zilzina could tell this was different. The cambion was tapping into that fire in anger. Honestly, maybe that's just what they needed right now.

Yulav groaned and took a step toward them. "Enough blubbering," she said and stretched her four arms. "I will feast now."

Slipping her new jacket off and handing it to Autumn, Zilzina stood and faced the hellspawn, dagger and pistol in hand. "Why come so far? It's not like demons to attack a city of this size, to risk angering the empire."

With a sneer that showed off its wicked teeth, Yulav answered. "You have no idea what you have, do you? She's special. Her blood is…" It inhaled deeply and grinned. "... unlike any I have ever tasted. And yours? Unique, though less so. I will take great pleasure in draining you both."

"Try it," Zilzina said, rolling up her left sleeve and drawing a thin line of blood from it with her dagger. The crowded design of tattoos started to hum and emit shadow.

"Are you so eager to give me a taste of your blood that you draw it for me?" mocked Yulav. "I will oblige, though I had thought to make this meal a slower, more evenly paced affair.

No matter, your power shall soon add to mine."

Power? No, this is a curse, Zilzina thought as the dark magic surged through her body. *Both of us are cursed.* She noticed a few embers floating through the air, emanating from Autumn, like the night they had met.

"Indeed, let's make this slow," spat the elf, her voice deepening into a chorused growl as the shadow spread from her arm across her body. "You do not deserve a quick death."

In a clash of hellspawn and shadow, Yulav and Zilzina attacked each other. The hunter jumped high over the demon's brutish attacks, swinging her dagger down to slash an arc into one of Yulav's upper arms. Two more arms returned a blow from the other side, which Zilzina flared her shadow to intercept, slowing them down just enough for her to dodge. As she slid away from the initial encounter, the hunter channeled the shadow from defense onto her blade, causing it to come alive with black flames that flickered soundlessly and emitted a heat so intense it felt cold, or perhaps a cold so intense it felt hot–the elf could never quite tell. Yulav hissed and stepped back, knowing how dangerous the black flames were.

Zilzina simply cocked an eyebrow over her ferociously glowing violet eyes and renewed her attack, wielding the deadly flame with reckless abandon. It was almost as dangerous to the wielder as the opponent. Almost. *Serah.*

Audrey. Autumn. They were worth the risk.

Her blade connected with one of Yulav's wrist, severing it instantly. The large, clawed hand skittered across the wood planked floor. Yulav roared and returned the injury with a double-fisted blow to Zilzina's side, sending her flying across the room. She had overextended to land the attack. Something inside her audibly snapped as the elf connected heavily with the wall, but she didn't have time to think about that now. The dark magic would keep her moving for the time being. Afterward though...

Yulav moved to pick up the hand, the tendrils of flesh already extending from each severed side toward each other. Truly this beast had an uncanny ability to heal. Zilzina welled up a black flame inside of her and breathed it out, withering the excised appendage before Yulav could reattach it. That was one arm down, though Zilzina could feel herself running out of energy to control the darkfire. If she went too far, it would totally consume her.

Yulav stood still for a moment and gritted its teeth. "You should not have done that," it said. Suddenly, its horns grew in size, as did its already monstrous form. Its now whip-like tail snapped out, lashing Zilzina across the face. With barely time to recover from the strike, Zilzina just made it out of the way of the charging hellspawn. It was faster now. Much faster. The demon's impact with the wall blew a person-sized hole straight through it, though it stopped its momentum.

Glancing from the shadowy form of the elf to the still immobile Autumn, Yulav changed tactics. It charged Autumn. Knowing full well it was a trap, Zilzina barreled into the demon's side, firing her pistol point-blank as she did so, but Yulav was ready. The gunshot was a grazing blow, far less severe than the full brunt of Yulav's three-armed attack that landed two solid punches and a grapple onto Zilzina's battered body. With great effort, Zilzina planted a boot on Yulav's chest and pushed back, breaking the grip and sliding across the floor to Autumn.

She was losing control of the darkflame.

Zilzina briefly considered just giving up, laying there and waiting for the end. Then her eyes met Autumn's again, and she knew she couldn't do that. As she rose, the faces of Serah's children flashed before her eyes. Then was Diona and her family, followed by Martha and Klaus. Finally, Autumn's mother, laying in the middle of their little cabin in the woods as Autumn's father feasted on her flesh.

No, I'm not done yet. Zilzina began a low chant as Yulav moved in to strike again. Her shadow formed into dark chains, wrapping quickly around the demon's three remaining hands. A spurt of blood erupted from her nose with the effort. Yulav strained for a moment before delivering a powerful kick to the elf's stomach. She'd tied the arm and forgotten the legs.

With a crunch, Zilzina crumpled against the glass clock face, cracks and blood spreading out from her impact. As Yulav approached slowly, knowing it had won, the elf scrambled frantically for her dagger, coughing up blood all the while. *So this is it,* she thought. *What a terrible ending.*

Yulav spit a glob of blood onto Zilzina's shirt and picked her up by the throat. "Utterly pathetic," the demon shouted, its voice raw with anger. "I will make you regret taking my hand!"

"Let her go," said Autumn shakily. She was standing now, leaning against the wall and steadying herself on one leg. In her trembling hand shook Zilzina's silvered dagger

"Oh, I'll be with you later. I'm taking my time with this one."

Darkness crept into the edges of Zilzina's vision as Yulav's grasp tightened. She had to do something. Anything. But she was so weak.

Suddenly, the pressure on the elf's neck loosened and she fell to the ground. Autumn was attacking the demon, slicing down her side with the dagger and being swatted away like a pest for her efforts. The damage was minimal, but Zilzina was free. Spotting her pistol, Zilzina grabbed it, slid a pair of silvered bullets down the chamber, and leveled it just as Yulav turned back to her. The demon was mid-roar. Zilzina's double-chambered shot caught it right in the back of the throat.

Silver was deadly to hellspawn, though one as strong as Yulav would take more than that to be killed. Still, the enormous beast clawed at its own throat, gurgling as the silver burned like acid there. The distraction was enough for Zilzina to crawl over to Autumn.

"Go," the elf managed between ragged breaths. "Get out of here. Hide. Serah can help you."

"Serah's alive? And no, I'm not leaving you." Autumn was standing now, ignoring the crippling pain in her leg.

"I can't beat her. Please, don't die here with me."

"I won't," Autumn replied. She turned to face the demon, who was still recovering from the throat shot. "Neither will you."

Heat poured forth from the girl in waves, sending ripples throughout the room. As flames started to form a few inches from Autumn's skin, smoke curled from her fingertips and the edges of her clothes. Within moments, an inferno seemed to engulf her and Zilzina, completely cutting them off from the rest of the world. From Yulav. Outside, the hellspawn screamed in a language neither of them understood. Its shrieks grew and grew with the intensity of the flames until suddenly it all stopped.

Silence and ash filled the air. The blackened floor trembled with instability as Zilzina gazed in awe to the black spot where Yulav had been. Nothing but ash was there now. Autumn turned to her sister, the fire still burning in her eyes, and offered a hand. Hesitantly, Zilzina took it.

"Are you...?" the elf began.

"I'm okay," said Autumn, helping the hunter to her feet. Her mangled leg seemed fully healed. "Let's go find Serah."

***

Out on the street, Autumn and Zilzina watched as the top of the clocktower buckled and crumbled in on itself. They'd only just made it into the shadows of one of the old trade district's many alleyways as a crowd began to form. The city guard was there as well, though they didn't seem to be looking for them. Everyone was murmuring and talking about the giant demon.

All at once, as the ash drifted down toward them, it began to snow.

"It's dead," Autumn muttered to herself, examining her hands. "I killed it."

"You did. You had to," replied Zilzina, who was leaning against a stack of crates and wincing.

"We have to get back. I don't have my mask."

"Don't worry about that now, just help me. We have to get back to Serah."

The pair limped through the back alleys of Sapoul,

dodging crowds and guards as they went. They were in poor shape, moving slowly, but the snow thickened into a storm, obscuring the vision of anyone who might see them. A bit of good luck at last.

The journey back to Serah's was a long one, but they were finally safe. Now it was time to deal with the consequences.

***

Autumn watched as Serah tended to Zilzina on the small bed. They'd returned and found her and the children hiding in the mirror room. Though it had been the hardest thing she'd ever done, Autumn had volunteered to move the bodies of the five slain children into the cellar so they could prepare them for a proper burial. Her new brothers and sisters, dead because of her–it was the least she could do. She'd only stopped to wretch once and then set to work. Now they were all together upstairs, safe. Yulav was dead. She'd killed the hellspawn.

It was the least she could do.

Serah's healing magic was impressive. She'd made sure Autumn was safe first before starting to stabilize Zilzina. The old woman's own wounds were bound with a blood-stained bandage but she insisted that she was fine.

"She'll be okay," Serah said at last, wiping sweat from her brow. "She just needs to rest now. We all do."

"I shouldn't be here," muttered Autumn, hiding her eyes. The other children were all looking at her. None of them had said a word since she'd returned. "I should go. This is all-"

A slap landed on Autumn's cheek, taking her by surprise. Serah followed it up with a hug and a firm shake. "Never say that again. Do you hear me? Not to me and especially not to her."

Autumn simply nodded and buried her face into Serah's shoulder. If she'd had any left, she would have shed a tear. "I didn't mean for any of this to happen."

"I know sweetie. Shh, sleep now. Everything will be alright."

***

"I can't stay here," Autumn said at last. She was sitting next to Zilzina, grey morning sunlight streaming in through the frosted window.

"I know," replied Zilzina, sitting up. It had been two days since the encounter with Yulav and she was just regaining her strength.

"It wouldn't be safe. For them."

"No, it wouldn't."

They sat quietly for a while, enjoying the sounds of Serah and the children preparing breakfast below. Everything had been somber, quieter the past few days, but things were getting... better.

"I'm not a child, you know," Autumn said.

"Yes, you are."

"I'm not like them."

"No, you're not like them."

"I can handle life on the road."

"I know you can," replied Zilzina, drawing her knees to her chest. "But it will be a hard life. You can handle it, but it's okay to hurt. We'll fix things, just you wait."

Autumn smiled for the first time since Yulav had attacked. "Yeah."

"Has Serah discovered anything about Otto?" continued Zilzina.

"Still ceramic, though she believes he's alive in there. Just has to find a way to get him out of it. Some sort of defensive technique."

"Well, she'll figure out a way. In the meantime," the elf said, inhaling deeply. "Breakfast smells delicious. And I need to get out of this bed."

"I know, you're starting to get as lazy as me," Autumn quipped.

The pair continued to banter like old times as they prepared for the day. As the sun rose, so did their spirits, and before long the house was filled with laughter again, though the sad silence always seemed to interject. It would take time to move on from what had happened.

***

Another few days passed. They kept busy with repairs to the

house and a memorial for the children who hadn't made it. Eventually, everything felt like it was returning to normal, though Autumn still saw Serah crying sometimes when she thought no one could see.

Esha and the others had started talking to Autumn. Slowly at first, but now they treated her like a sister again. Autumn was happy to know they forgave her, even if she couldn't forgive herself. She and Zilzina would have to leave soon, and she didn't want to make things even more painful by laying that burden on them though. They deserved to be happy.

One morning, the silver haired, violet eyed elf walked up to the roof where Esha and Autumn were reading. She was in full travel attire. With a nod, Autumn stood and offered Esha the book she'd been reading.

"Here, this one is really good," the cambion said, handing the novel over. "We can talk about it when we visit again."

"Please come back soon!" Esha squealed, hugging her.

"As soon as we can," replied Zilzina, ruffling the girl's hair and turning to leave.

Autumn followed, waving. "Be back before you know it."

THE HUNGER WILL CONTINUE IN…

WINTER'S ASHES

SEPTEMBER 2022

Join the mailing list at HungerOfTheAbyss.com for updates, extras, merchandise, and a free novella.

ABOUT THE AUTHOR

Luke Hoffman is an author and game designer hailing from Sacramento, CA. His works include *The Scarlet Bride; or a Bloodstained Romance* and *Aeon*, as well as the *Hunger of the Abyss* series, which was written largely at his favorite local haunt, Bottle and Barlow.

Made in United States
Orlando, FL
02 December 2023

39981904R00139